MW01487930

Sacred Honor

Jim Dulski

To my friend Patty

Jim Dulski

Dedication

Thank you to my wife Barb and family,
Jim (Alexis, Noah and Eden), Bill (Angela), John and Mike.

And to all those people who helped and encouraged me to
keep going with this project.

Table of Contents

CHAPTER ONE

It is our duty still to endeavor to avoid war; but if it shall actually take place, no matter by whom brought on, we must defend ourselves. If our house be on fire, without inquiring whether it was fired from within or without, we must try to extinguish it.

Thomas Jefferson

HOW COULD IT HAVE COME TO THIS? PEN IN HAND, sitting at his desk in Austin, Texas, governor James Walter pondered the question and the enormous decision and undertaking that he was about to make. His thoughts drifted to others that found themselves in similar circumstances. By signing the document before him, he would set in motion events that would profoundly change the course of the United States, and cement his place in history. Men such as Thomas Jefferson and Benjamin Franklin are remembered as heroes, while Jefferson

Davis and Robert E. Lee are regarded as villains. What would his place in history be patriot or traitor?

Looking out his office window he could see the looming clouds gathering in the western sky, the pending storm… *How prophetic,* he thought. *What has brought us as a people to this moment that will ultimately alter our future and possibly lead to a second civil war?*

He reads the words of the document that he helped to draft… carefully crafted words in the style of the founders, updated in modern language but reflecting the same grievances of those that existed over 200 years ago. It begins.

When in the course of history, it becomes essential for a people to terminate the bonds that join them, it is essential to proclaim the injustices that have caused them to such severance.

"Everything is ready Governor."

Ron Thompson was Jim Walter's right hand man and life-long friend. He had been with him from the start of his 20 year political career; beginning as an advisor on his first campaign for Mayor of Dallas, through the state legislature, all the way to the governor's mansion, his loyalty was unquestionable, but that loyalty would now be tested like never before.

"The State National Guard and militia units are standing by to seal the borders and close off all the roads, airports, train and bus stations, and guard the gulf coastline."

Poised above the parchment pen still in hand Jim Walter says nothing, only slowly nodding his head in acknowledgement, he continues reading.

We must reaffirm the incontrovertible truths of the civil liberties of life and self-determination bestowed upon us by our creator. That just governments be established by the governed to secure these liberties. That when such government becomes detrimental to such liberties, it becomes the duty of the people to dissolve such government and re-establish justice.

Wisdom dictates that governments not be abolished without just cause, but when such abuses of power become destructive to the good of the governed, it is the right of the people to eradicate such tyranny and provide new safe guards for their future preservation. Let the facts show that the people of Texas do not enter into such action without just cause.

Experience hath shown that even under the best forms of government those entrusted with power have, in time, and by slow operation, perverted in into tyranny.

Thomas Jefferson

Jim Dulski

In the Oval Office, 1,500 miles away, President Omar Brown sits behind the Resolute (see note in references) desk and reads the headline of tomorrows' Washington Post.
PRESIDENT SIGNS EXECUTIVE ORDER OUTLAWING PRIVATE FIREARM OWNERSHIP

"Mr. President," Chief of Staff Meyer Epstein spoke in his normal matter of fact tone,

"I would be remiss in my duty as your political advisor to not attempt to dissuade you from pursuing this course."

"What is the problem Meyer? This has been our goal all along."

"Yes sir, but it was to be achieved through a slow process of attrition… a constant erosion of the Second Amendment by regulation, taxation, legislation and registration which would ultimately lead to confiscation."

"I know Meyer, but this latest school shooting is like a gift from the gods, the whole country is focused on it, we must take advantage of this opportunity."

Epstein thought for a moment before making his reply, finding it difficult to disagree with the President, any President, but understanding the personality of this man whose faith lies in his ideology.

"Mr. President… the polls suggest that if this administration continues on this course, we will be faced with a further divided Congress and the possibility of insurrection and open rebellion."

"Meyer, there's no going back now. The Constitution, Supreme Court and Congress be damned. Now is the time that the progressive agenda must be forced upon the American public!"

President Brown pondered what Epstein had said. *Will this be what defines my legacy*, he thought? *Healthcare and immigration reform will be forgotten and become mere footnotes of our achievements. How will I be remembered? Will I be compared to Abraham Lincoln, or to Benedict Arnold?* His only solace was the knowledge that history is written by the victors.

"We must succeed! Have all the arrangements been made?"

Epstein knew it was futile to argue further.

"Yes sir, everything is in place. All contingency plans stand at the ready to be implemented. We have control of the media and internet. All branches of the military have cancelled all leaves and are under orders of the commander- in -chief to quell any public insurrection, calling National Guard units to assist in implementing martial law, if necessary.

The FBI and ATF are on alert to work with state, county and local governments to utilize registration data bases to confiscate all weapons that are not voluntarily surrendered. FEMA has been notified to stand by to implement emergency plans to commandeer the railroads and coordinate with Homeland Security to transport insurgents to strategically located designated military bases, airports and stadiums to be used as internment camps, and the UN has pledged to send in peace keeping forces if required".

One man with courage is a majority.

Thomas Jefferson

"Governor," Thompson had never seen his friend so despondent.

"Are you all right?" he asked.

Head down, Jim Walter again only nodded and read on.

The President has refused to abide by the most sacred laws of the land by subverting and circumventing the United States Constitution.

He has abused the powers granted to his office to bypass Congress.

He has coerced legislation despite the will of the people.

He has recklessly pursued economic policies that brought this nation to the verge of bankruptcy.

He has engaged in the drafting and signing of treaties with foreign governments without the consent of Congress.

He has refused to recognize the sovereignty of the states to enforce the laws of their constitutions.

He has caused the people to be taxed without consent to support the growth of government and not the betterment of the people.

He has abolished the right of the people to self-defense by refusing to recognize the authority of the Supreme Court and the second amendment of the Bill of Rights.

To the people of Texas, these repeated transgressions and disregard for the rule of law are tantamount to treason to such degree that we formally declare our independence. We therefore pledge our Sacred Honor to the sovereign Republic Of Texas.

Jim Walter's hand hovered over the document. His head still lowered, he again pondered his question: How could it have come to this? Ever since reconstruction, our ancestors predicted another Civil War would occur, not to preserve the principal that all men, black or white, are created equal, or resurrect the practice of slavery, but that this time it will be fought to prevent a tyrannical government from enslaving all of its citizens! A government that rules, not by a representative congress of the people, but by the executive order of a dictatorship!

What fools we thought men like Sinclair Lewis, whose 1935 book "It Can't Happen Here" to make such predictions of the rise of a totalitarian state, "crazies, gun nuts, extremists;"

how we laughed at the citizen militias and doomsday preppers while they made their plans, for this truly could never happen here in America. Now we must call upon these same people to help us in the struggle to prevent the very thing that we scoffed at them for believing. God really does have a sense of irony!

His thoughts again drifted off to better times when he was a boy, when he and Ron Thompson would spend their days fishing on the Little River. "That cat sure put up one hell of a fight," he whispered to himself as he remembered the 12 pound lunker he hooked on a flat worm and spoon.

How much simpler life was then. They never would have dreamt that one day they would be in this position. *What a fight that was , up, down, left, right, reel it in then let it run, it tried to get into the remains of semi submerged tree branch, but I was able to pull him back upstream and away from that obstacle only to have it run for the rocks downstream. That fish had lived in that river for God knows how many years and knew it like I knew the back county of Bell County; it had survived many a fight such as this. Forty five minutes later, his battle scars were evident when I finally pulled him onto the bank. "What a war" I* thought then… little did I know what war lay ahead.

He signed.

James Douglas Walter

President; Republic Of Texas

Standing up he looked at the worried face of his friend. "Ron, when this is over, let's go fishing."

CHAPTER TWO

After a shooting spree, they always want to take the guns away from the people who didn't do it. I sure as hell wouldn't want to live in a society where the only people allowed guns are the police and the military.

William S Burroughs

THE ALARM RANG LOUD IN DENNIS COLEMAN'S BED-room at 5:00 a.m.; in one swift motion he instinctively swung his hand to hit the snooze button and began his morning routine. Sitting up to light a smoke he stared at the end of the cigarette and gathered his thoughts... *another day of bullshit!* Inhaling deeply he stood to stretch his six foot frame. *Coffee, I need coffee!* Showered and dressed, he slowly walked down the stairs, smelling the heady aroma of the brewing coffee; pouring a hot cup he took a small sip and then one big gulp...*God damn that's good!* Looking out the window, he could see that the morning paper was lying in its usual place at the bottom of the stoop. Quickly stepping out into the cold of a March Chicago morning, he retrieved the paper and even more quickly ran back into the warmth of the house. Refilling his cup, Dennis sat down to read the paper. Partly cloudy, flurries, high 35, low 27, he had not yet read the headline. Turning to the sports, Hawks and Bulls both won, and the Sox pitching staff is looking good in spring training. Finally turning to the headline, his cup fell from his hand.

PRESIDENT'S ORDER OUTLAWS GUNS

He ran to turn on the TV… *nothing on FOX, CNN, NBC, CBS…every channel had the same image of the podium with the Presidential Seal and a bulletin stating that the President would address the nation at 10:00 a.m.* Back to the newspaper, he continued reading.

President Brown signs executive order banning all civilian gun ownership. Citing the recent school shootings and the rise in homicides in cities such as Chicago, President Brown stated,

"We as a people can no longer tolerate the carnage that is taking place on the streets of our nation, therefore, I have taken the following necessary steps. First, I have signed an executive order that prohibits all private civilian gun ownership of any kind."

Leaving the paper, he quickly dialed Miguel's number. One, two, three… after four rings, an angry, groggy voice yelled, "**WHAT?**"

Miguel Torres was the youngest son of an immigrant father of Cuban descent, who had escaped communist Cuba with his family, crossing 90 miles of water in a small boat. Miguel, too, was a determined hardworking man, strong and tough, he was just as quick to cuss as he was to laugh and did not like being woken up!

"**Mike, have you seen the paper?**"

"**What fucking time is it?**"

"**Never mind that! Have you seen the paper?**"

"**It's five fucking thirty,**" came an even more angry reply.

"**Wake up asshole!** They did it, they banned guns!"

"**What?**"

"**Turn on the news; they've taken over the media.**"

Still half asleep, Miguel paused, his mind spinning. He had known this day would come, but now it was here! His father told him stories of helping his grandfather bury their weapons in the cane fields when Castro came to power in Cuba back in 1959. He had been warned about the signs that lead up to the revolution, he had seen those signs and planned for it, but was he prepared?

"Mike, You still there?"

"Yeah. Get your shit and meet me down the road."

Without saying goodbye, Dennis ended the call. He knew what this meant, a pre-planned meeting place in the forest preserve in Will County just outside of Chicago.

Gathering his weapons, ammunition and supplies, he concealed them in towels and blankets and hid them beneath the false floor in the back of his pick up as fast as he could. He placed his fishing equipment on top as camouflage and headed out to meet Miguel and the others in the woods. It was time to prepare for the long ride to Arkansas to rendezvous with other KGC sentinels.

We shall defend our island, whatever the cost may be, we shall fight on the beaches, we shall fight on the landing grounds, we shall fight in the fields and in the streets, we shall fight in the hills, we shall never surrender.

Winston Churchill

Surveying the landscape, Texas National Guard General Joseph Scott appraised the strategic placement of the obstacles required to repel an invading force. Joe was no stranger to war. As a Colonel serving in Desert Shield and Desert Storm, as well as two tours of duty in Afghanistan, he knew that he could be faced with the unenviable task of defending multiple fronts from superior, overwhelming forces. Having studied military history and tactics at West Point, he understood the weaknesses and shortcomings of the French Maginot line that could not stop the Germans, and the Atlantic wall devised by a military genius such as Rommel, defenses that could not stop the allied forces from establishing a beachhead in WWII. "I'm being ordered to do the impossible," he thought to himself. Napoleon, Hitler… No army had been able to fight a war on two fronts throughout the history of warfare, but Joe knew the tactics of General George Crain, the man he would be up against and he had a few tricks up his sleeve.

The whole aim of practical politics is to keep the populace alarmed (and hence clamorous to be led to safety) by menacing it with an endless series of hobgoblins, all of them imaginary.

H.L Mencken

"Ladies and Gentlemen, the President of the United States!" Flanked by the American flag on both sides, President Brown approached the podium bearing the seal of his office.

"My fellow Americans, in light of the recent tragedy, in which 12 innocent children were senselessly gunned down, and the inability of the congress to quickly act to avoid such further tragedies from occurring in the future, I have decided to take the following measures."

"First, today I have signed an executive order, banning the possession of all firearms and ammunition by all private citizens not affiliated with law enforcement or the military."

"Second, all citizens will be required to voluntarily surrender all firearms and ammunition to your local authorities within 48 hours, or face criminal prosecution in special courts by judges appointed by the department of Homeland Security."

"Third, the bureau of Alcohol, Tobacco and Firearms has been empowered to seize all state and local databases listing firearm owners and ammunition purchases to identify, locate and confiscate these weapons, and arrest, detain and prosecute anyone who resists."

"Fourth, demonstrations contrary to supporting these policies will not be tolerated, and protesters will be indefinitely detained until such time as their cases can be adjudicated in Homeland Security courts. Fifth, all state and local authorities are hereby directed to assist and coordinate with ATF and Homeland Security forces to implement these orders."

"And finally, habeas corpus will not apply in cases brought before these courts. Again, let me be perfectly clear. All firearms of any kind, including hand guns, rifles, shotguns, from muzzle loaders to BB guns, designed for any purpose, are hereby outlawed for private ownership. Thank You."

"Ladies and Gentlemen... that was the President of the United States."

Courage is being scared to death... and saddling up anyway.

John Wayne

The traffic was unusually light for this time of day. Driving south on I-55 out of Chicago toward the meeting place in the woods, Dennis Coleman's thoughts again wandered to the events of the day and what lay ahead. *So much to do in so little time, but above all he must keep a clear mind.* Looking at his speedometer he realized he was speeding. *Be careful,* he thought, *the last thing you need is to be pulled over.* Slowing down, Dennis kept a watchful eye out for state police cruisers and was careful to drive at the posted speed. Pulling into a truck stop to fuel up and get some breakfast, he took a seat at an empty table near the window and again contemplated the trip ahead and what he must do.

His thoughts were broken when the waitress strolled up to his table. "Coffee?"

Dennis glanced up at her, good looking woman, 30ish, blonde, nice figure. On any other day he might try to strike up a conversation with her, but not today!

"Black" he replied.

Watching as the waitress walked away, he gazed around the dinner and could not help but notice that it was strangely quiet; all the other customers had the same expressions on their faces... *a look of numbness, as if they all had just heard some terrible news and were all deep in some serious thought. Was this how people looked on the day Pearl Harbor was bombed, or the day that President Kennedy was killed?* It reminded him of another day he had seen that same blank look on people's faces, that day was September 11, 2001.

"Ready to order?" The waitress asked, as she placed the coffee cup on the table.

Without thinking or looking up,

"Two eggs up with bacon, hash browns, and white toast" he replied in a monotone voice. Coleman felt like he was on autopilot, reviewing the list in his mind... Weapons, ammunition, maps, clothing, camping gear and supplies... check. Fuel, cash, cigarettes... check. Batteries, flashlight, radio, matches, flint..., all in the bug-out bag. Miguel has the tent and shovels. *What am I forgetting?*

Going over it again and again, he hadn't even realized that his breakfast was now on the table. Taking a bite of the eggs, Dennis returned to studying the faces of the people in the diner. *What were they thinking? What were they feeling? Were their thoughts the same as his? What was it he was feeling?* Up until now, this had all seemed like a game of army that we played as children, planning and preparing for this day, hoping it would never happen but fearing that it would. The thought hit him like a hammer…*fear*, that's what you're feeling! The same fear that the colonists had when they fought the British…the same fear that the soldiers in the landing craft felt at Normandy Beach. But was it fear of dying or fear of the lack of courage to follow through?

He again contemplated the people's faces as if he himself were searching for something but did not know what. Scanning the room, his eyes focused on an older man wearing a ball cap, who appeared to be staring out the window at what seemed like nothing, his head was turned at such an angle that Dennis could see an American flag pin, but could not make out what was written on the cap.

"Was everything OK??"

Dennis looked down at his empty plate, and it occurred to him that he could not remember eating a single bite.

"Fine"

"Can I get you anything else??"

"No, just the check"

The waitress ripped the check from her pad, laid it on the table, and turned and walked away. *Nice legs,* he thought as he watched her disappear though the kitchen doors. Gulping down the last bit of coffee he looked down at the check and read what was written on the stub…

Jill 708-555-1035. Looking up, he could see Jill's face smiling at him though the kitchen window. Dennis felt good for the first time that day.

Standing up to leave, he reached into his wallet, pulled out a twenty dollar bill and laid it on top of the check with the now missing stub and walked toward the door As Dennis approached the old man who was still staring out of the window, the old man broke his gaze, turned and looked Dennis directly in the eye; nodding his head, his expression had changed from one of melancholy to that of stern determination. Dennis returned the nod of the head and could now see what was on the man's cap, an image of a flying eagle with an American flag in its talons and the words "These Colors Don't Run"

Power corrupts, and absolute power corrupts absolutely.

Lord Acton

Back in the Oval Office, President Brown and Meyer Epstein sat comfortably on the sofa. "Well Meyer… what do you think we should expect?"

"Mr. President, I believe that this action will be well received by your base," Epstein replied matter-of-factly. "The governors of New York, Illinois and California have already made statements of support, the UN has also released a statement upholding it as a bold move toward the future," Epstein continued, "and except for FOX News, which has been censored from the air, all the major news outlets are preparing commentaries and editorials of praise." "However, as expected, the right wing is screaming bloody murder, the Speaker of the House is preparing articles of impeachment, and the moderates are divided. Essentially, we stand at the threshold of revolution, and the next 24 to 48 hours will determine if the rest of the country capitulates, or if we enter into a second civil war of outright rebellion or guerrilla warfare."

As Brown pondered his options, the silence was broken by the ring of Epstein's cell phone…

"Epstein… when?"

Epstein hung up the phone.

"Sir… we have word that the Governor of Texas has requested air time on all local television stations in Texas to make a statement."

"When?" A look of concern crossed Brown's face.

"Now. Turn on the TV"

Flanked by Texas state flags on either side, Governor Jim Walter sat behind a large wooden desk.

"Fellow Texans," he began. "In response to the actions taken this day by the President, the Texas Legislature has convened in emergency session and resolved to sever allegiance to the United States of America and declare the sovereign Republic of Texas. At this moment, a document declaring our independence, and the grievances which have caused such separation, are being transmitted to the White House."

Right on cue the fax machine began to print out the document.

"This document should not be construed as a declaration of hostilities," Walter continued, "but a realization that two peoples of differing cultures should separate to a peaceful coexistence. However, as a precaution, all units of the Texas Guard, as well as local law enforcement and citizen militia units have been placed on standby alert in the event that the borders of the Republic of Texas are violated by any invading force. Any and all necessary means at my disposal will be employed to repel such force. Defensive positions and check points have been established at Interstate highways and all major roads that intersect with the Texas borders. The Texas constitution shall remain in force with the following exceptions: all citizens who wish to remain citizens of the United States may leave and will be allowed to freely cross over into the United States, but will be required to obtain a passport to re-enter. For security purposes, reentry may be denied. Commerce will continue as usual with the following exceptions: all U.S. dollars will be converted to Texas bank currency, which will be backed by reserves of gold, silver, and petroleum. All goods entering or leaving by truck, rail, or air must be inspected and have proper documentation issued by the Texas department of commerce. In closing, we shall endeavor to make this transition as smooth as possible. Please contact your local government administrators and law enforcement officials for assistance with any questions that may arise. With your patience and the help of God, we shall persevere to become the great nation envisioned by our forefathers. May God bless you… and may GOD BLESS TEXAS!"

CHAPTER THREE

Texas will again lift its head and stand among the nations. It ought to do so, for no country upon the globe can compare with it in natural advantages.

Sam Houston

JOE SCOTT STOOD AT THE TABLE SURVEYING THE MAP that was laid out before him. Knowing George Crain the way he did, he knew that his whole military philosophy centered on identifying an enemies' weakness to exploit it to strategic advantage. He also knew that if he could create the illusion of weakness, he could take advantage of Crain's weakness… his ego! It would be essential to induce an attack on terrain of their choosing.

"General." Joe Scott's adjutant, Colonel William Baker, stood at attention. "We have secured the army bases of Forts

Hood and Bliss, and Fort Sam Houston has been ordered to turn over control to the Texas Guard. The air bases of Brooks City, Dyess, Goodfellow, Lackland, Laughlin, Randolph and Sheppard have all checked in."

A tough Texan through and through, Baker was long and lean, very competent and extremely efficient.

"Naval air stations at Fort Worth, Corpus Christie and Kingsville have also been secured; all military personnel who wish to remain loyal to the United States have been restricted to quarters until arrangements are made for transport out of Texas."

Joe Scott sat quietly listening to Baker's progress report. "Have we established our defensive positions?" Scott asked."

"Sir, all 254 county militia units have checked in and all roads along the borders leading out of Texas are secured. Tank traps are being constructed and anti-personnel obstacles and decoys are being deployed. As ordered, roadblock checkpoints have been established on interstate highways I-10, I-20, I-30 and 35, and I-40 and 44 along the borders."

"Are our plans for operation Soft Spot being implemented?"

"Yes sir. We have attempted to create the illusion of a weak defensive posture along the Louisiana border north of I-10, with units of citizen county militia occupying front line positions to draw an attack. Concealed mobile armored units supported by infantry have been placed at pre-planned strategic points approximately 1 to 1 and a half miles, depending on the terrain behind this line with batteries of M-102 105mm, Howitzer artillery units have taken up positions behind the armored units. All airports, railroads and ports of entry or exit are being manned by elements of local law enforcement supported by Texas Guardsmen, and county militia."

"Good. What about air defense?"

"With your permission, we wish to deploy M48 Chaparral missiles as well as M163 VAD mobile anti-aircraft units around Austin."

"Permission granted." Scott detected a sense of apprehension in Baker's tone. "Anything else Colonel?"

"Yes sir, may I speak freely?"

"At ease Bill."

"What the hell are we doing Joe? Are we actually preparing to wage war against our own country?" Baker's voice rose. "Joe, we swore an oath and now we are going to fire on our own people... this is crazy!"

Scott sat quietly for a moment before replying. "Well Bill, I'm sure that the colonists must have shared the same anxieties. Even though King George taxed them, and refused to let the colonies have their own representation or self-government, and tried to disarm them, they still had loyalty to the crown. Eventually they had no choice. This President has done basically the same thing so I don't see where we have much of a choice either."

Baker's voice was now more animated. "I understand that, but couldn't a political solution… some sort of compromise be made that would avert secession?"

"I wish it could Bill, but even if one was found we would be ignoring history. World War II could have been avoided if we stood up to Hitler when the Germans marched into Munich. Appeasement only makes the aggressor more aggressive. By continuing to ignore the lessons of history, I think it was inevitable that it would come to this." Scott's voice became stern. "What we fail to understand is that this is not about the safety and security of the private citizen. It's just the ploy they are using to advance the agenda toward changing our representative republic to a communist-socialist form of government."

Scott rose from his chair and became more animated. "Bill, this is about preserving the Constitution and our way of life. The Declaration of Independence tells us that whenever any form of government becomes destructive to these ends, it is the right of the people to alter or to abolish it, and to institute new government!" Yes, we swore an oath!," Scott said as he slammed his closed fist onto the desk top. "The same oath that the President swore-to preserve, protect and defend the

Constitution from all enemies, foreign and domestic. What we failed to realize was that, by his own actions, our own commander in chief violated that oath and became that domestic enemy."

Baker stood motionless, thoughtfully considering the words that Scott had spoken. "I know all that Joe, but I can't help having mixed emotions. I mean, if an attack takes place we will be firing on soldiers that are wearing the same uniforms as us. And what if we fail? We'll be branded as traitors, court marshaled for treason and imprisoned for life-if not shot!" Baker was now becoming emotional. "What will happen to our wives and children? Will they be interred? Will our homes and property be confiscated? How will they live, how will they survive?"

Scott came around the desk and placed his hand on Baker's shoulder. "I understand what you're feeling Bill, I feel the same way. But ask yourself how will they live and survive in a world where there is no longer a country that they can be free? Free to speak their minds, free to defend themselves, free to make their own decisions and be safe from government intrusion into everything that they do? Or would you prefer that they live in a world where the government can dictate everything they do, down to the size and amount of a soft drink you can have like they do in New York City? We are not the only ones who have had these feelings Bill. Over two hundred years ago, men like Jefferson, Adams, Hamilton and Madison risked their lives and fortunes for essentially the same reasons, so I'm proud to say we're in pretty good company!"

Baker slowly nodded his head. He turned to leave, and then stopped. Turning back and raising his eyes to look Scott directly in the face, he grinned. "Have you been practicing that speech?"

"Yeah... how was it?"

"Not bad!"

The woods are lovely, dark and deep. But I have promises to keep, and miles to go before I sleep.

Robert Frost

"It'll be spring soon," Dennis thought to himself. Driving off the main street onto a dirt service road that paralleled the old Illinois & Michigan canal, he had to be careful not to miss the turn off onto the forest trail that led to the secluded meeting spot used by fisherman along the Des Plaines River. Dennis loved this time of year, a new beginning, everything soon to be turning green. He loved to fish, to quietly sit and think about everything and nothing while enjoying nature. It was on one of those slow fishing days about ten years ago that he decided to do a little exploring. Venturing into the woods, he discovered the small natural cave that cut into a hillside. Because of the small opening and the trees and brush concealing it, it was difficult to see unless you came right upon it. Peering inside it was completely dark. Taking out his keychain flashlight, he could see that it was about fifteen to twenty yards deep and approximately twelve feet wide. It looked as though some small animals had used it as a refuge, but there were no signs of any human presence. *What a perfect hiding place*, he thought at the time.

Slowing down around a curve in the road, he found the trail he was looking for on the right, just past the fallen sycamore tree. Turning onto the trail, he could see fresh tire tracks in the muddy path. Stopping the pickup and rolling down his window, he gave one short beep of his horn and listened for the reply. After a couple of seconds he heard the response-two short beeps, a pause, followed by one slightly longer one, it was Miguel. Dennis slowly drove on another fifty yards, until he saw the back of the box truck parked in the middle of the trail. Miguel stepped out of the truck and greeted Dennis.

"Where have you been?" Miguel asked in an angry voice.

"I had to stop for gas, cigarettes and get something to eat."

"We have a lot of work to do," Miguel said. "Let's get unloaded."

Dennis and Miguel started up the trail toward the small cave, where they met two other sentinels, John and Don, who had already unloaded their guns, ammunition, and supplies. Dennis greeted John and Don with a wave of his hand.

"Can you believe they're doing this?" Don questioned.

"What the hell do you think we been preparing for?" Miguel growled.

"I just never thought they would go through with it! They had to know that people wouldn't take this lying down and there would be resistance." Don shot back.

"Of course they knew! They don't care! These people don't think like you and I, they're hell-bent on implementing socialism on America, and they see this as their opportunity." Now Miguel was really angry.

"Do you think Stalin cared when he disarmed the Russian people in 1929? No! And 20 million dissidents were rounded up and exterminated! Did Mao care when 20 million Chinese were killed from 1948 to 52? Hitler established gun control in 1938 and another defenseless 20 million Jews and political dissidents were eliminated!" There was no stopping Miguel now, he was on a roll. "That's 60 million so far, and we haven't even mentioned Turkey, Guatemala, Uganda, Cambodia, and Cuba, where another 3 to 4 million unarmed Armenians, Christians, Mayan Indians and other political prisoners and educated people were exterminated. That's 64 million people in the 20th century alone! Shall I continue, or can we get back to work now and hit the road?"

Without saying a word, the group went back to their task of loading the stores of weapons and supplies into the cave and concealing the entrance before heading out for Arkansas.

A free America... means just this: individual freedom for all, rich or poor, or else this system of government we call democracy is only an expedient to enslave man to the machine and make him like it.

Frank Lloyd Wright

President Brown and Meyer Epstein sat quietly, each waiting for the other to speak first. After a few awkward moments Epstein finally broke the silence.

"Mr. President." Epstein handed the faxed declaration to Brown.

"I'm not going to like this am I?" Brown asked sarcastically. "I'm pretty sure you're going to hate it, sir."

With a blank expression Brown began reading. Epstein watched as the president's eyes traveled left to right across the page. A look of fury crossed Brown's face.

"Treason, he's seceding from the union, and he's accusing *me* of treason! Get that son of a bitch on the phone!" Brown screamed!

"Yes sir." Epstein picked up the phone and instructed the Secretary to contact the governor of Texas.

"Just who the hell does he think he is to accuse the president of the United States of treason?"

Epstein had never seen the President so angry. "You need to remain presidential sir," said Epstein reassuringly. His attempt to calm Brown was interrupted when the secretary announced on the intercom that the governor of Texas was on the line. Brown pressed the speaker button and heard the familiar voice of Jim Walter.

"What can I do for you Mr. President?" Walter said in his Texas drawl.

"Don't give me that shit Jim!" Brown yelled. "Just what the hell do you think you're doing?"

"I'm representing the will of the people of Texas, but with all due respect sir, I might ask you the same question." Walter replied calmly.

"How dare you accuse the President of the United States of treason!"

"How would you have me term it Mr. President?" Walter's voice was now rising. "Not only have you repealed the Second Amendment, but to enforce this action you have nullified the first amendment by subverting the press, prohibiting speech and assembly to protest. You've ordered the military and law enforcement to ignore the fourth amendment by allowing warrantless searches and seizures of private property. You've rendered void the rights and protections of those accused of a crime, and deny bail, nullifying the fifth, sixth, seventh and eighth amendment's. By your actions, and not by the amending powers of Congress, you have for all intents and purposes shredded the Bill of Rights. I could have also accused you of violating your oath of office and conspiracy." A hint of sarcasm was now in Walter's tone. "I suppose I could have charged you with sedition instead of treason, but I wasn't sure if you had a dictionary handy."

Epstein was now waving his hands motioning for the president to calm down but Brown was now irate; nobody spoke to him like this!

"Don't you propose to lecture me, how many have to be killed before…"

"Before what?" Walter interrupted. "Before you enforce the laws that are already in effect, before you protect our borders and no longer allow criminals, murderers, and drug dealers to enter the country with impunity?"

"Just how many kids have to be killed, Governor, before we take action?" Brown countered, trying to yell over Walter's voice.

"Who's bullshitting who now Mr. President? Disarming this country has been part of your socialist agenda from day one, and you couldn't give a rat's ass how many kids are killed that furthers that goal."

His face covered in sweat and turning red, Brown was livid. He was not used to being debated in this fashion.

"Governor, I have sat with the families and loved ones of those who have been killed by gun violence. I've felt their pain and witnessed their tears, I've cried with them."

Again Walter interrupted. "Yes Mr. President, I've seen how you step over the bodies that you and your kind have caused to die to get in front of a television camera and embrace those grieving people with your crocodile tears."

"How dare you speak to me in this manner!" Brown screamed. "You will speak to me with the respect that I deserve!"

"Mr. President, I am showing you exactly the amount of respect that you deserve. None!"

Brown was beside himself, this was the last straw. Now howling at the top of his lungs he shouted, "Governor, let me be clear, we shall fundamentally change this country by conquest or consent and if you continue on this course you will face the full force of the United States government and its military!"

"Mr. President let me be clear. If you continue on this course you will have more on your hands to deal with than just the Republic of Texas. Good day sir."

Leaning against his desk, a still fuming President Brown stood motionless staring at the now silent phone. After a moment he fell back into his chair and his gaze fell on Meyer Epstein who was sitting on the couch with his head buried in his hands.

"What's wrong Meyer?" Brown asked.

"I hope he wasn't recording that!"

Back in Austin, Jim Walter hung up the phone, grinning he looked into the ashen face of Ron Thompson.

"I think that went well," he said.

CHAPTER FOUR

Educate and inform the whole mass of the people... They are the only sure reliance for the preservation of our liberty.

Thomas Jefferson

JILL RILEY APPROACHED THE OLD MAN THAT WAS SITting at the table. "You want more coffee dad?"

The old man was still looking out the window. "No thanks honey, you about ready to go?"

"Just about," she replied, "I'll meet you outside." Jill walked back into the kitchen to finish closing out her receipts after another long midnight shift at the truck stop. Counting out her tips, her concentration kept being interrupted with the thoughts of that tall man who she served breakfast to earlier. He seemed so preoccupied…she wondered if he was troubled with the same problem that was bothering her father after hearing the news that the government was beginning confiscating firearms?

Jill worried about her dad. He was a tough old bird, retired from the Marine Corps as a Master sergeant having served two tours in Viet Nam. Tommy "Gun" Riley was a Semper FI, always faithful, an old school, tough-as-nails patriot who had served his country with distinction and been awarded a purple heart after being wounded during battle.

A loving father, but also a strictly by the book man, dad always knew what to do in any situation, whenever she had a problem he would tell her "Honey, you have to decide to advance, retreat or stand your ground." But today he seemed unsure, as if that philosophy had somehow failed him. The only other time Jill had seen her father like this was when her mother passed away - he seemed almost lost, not knowing how to separate the emotions from the tactical training which were the guiding principles of his life.

Having finished her receipts, Jill walked out of the truck stop into the cool March morning air. Looking around, she noticed that dad wasn't parked in his usual spot. Finally, she spotted the familiar front of his Ford pickup, parked alongside the diesel pumps where an eighteen wheeler was fueling up. Although he was cordial to people, dad was not the type that would just engage in idle conversation; however, today he and the truck driver seemed to be involved in a serious discussion.

Not wanting to interrupt their discussion, Jill walked straight to the right side of the pickup and slid into the passenger seat. Inside the cab, the warm air from the heater was comforting compared to the 30 degree temperature outside. Not knowing how long this discussion would last, she relaxed into the seat and turned on the radio, and immediately was hearing the voice of the newscaster who was busy reporting the current events.

"This is Craig Stephens reporting from Washington, where President Brown, citing the most recent school shooting tragedy, has signed an executive order outlawing all private firearm ownership. The ban is effective immediately; all citizens are required to turn over any type of weapon, as well as ammunition, to local law enforcement within 48 hours. Noncompliance will result in confiscation by force, and anyone who does not cooperate will be subject to harsh penalties which include detainment and arrest by Homeland security, and prosecution in special firearm courts. The President also announced that any demonstrations of resistance or protest will not be tolerated and will also be subject to prosecution."

The voice of the anchorman now came on the radio. "Craig… this is Mathew Krys with NSMBA in New York. I have to say that I personally felt a thrill in my spine when I heard the announcement and I applaud the President's actions and believe this is long overdue, but what is the reaction on the street?"

"Well Matt... in the wake of the most recent school tragedy, everyone that we have interviewed has been very positive and welcomed this executive order with open arms!"

Jill knew propaganda when she heard it and turned off the radio. She turned on the CB to listen to the trucker chatter.

"This here's Road Ranger, south bound on double nickel headed toward the Big Arch. We got a military carrier full of soldier boys with a Boy Scout escort with their disco lights on north bound headed toward Chi-town... looks like they mean business." "I heard that Ranger... Bulldog Bob here, west bound on 80 headed for Omaha... word's the same all over from sea to shining sea... soldiers, with Smokey's and fly's in the sky... we got city kitties and local yokels all advertising!"

"Watch your words there neighbor Bob... these boys got their ears on... they're settin' up Check Point Charley's and using Kojacks with Kodak's looking to bust anyone with a pop gun!"

"10-4 Ranger... I hear tell outta Big –D and cow town that Texas has closed its borders. What's up with that? Come back."

Jill's ears were glued to the CB; she had hardly acknowledged that her father had gotten behind the wheel.

"10-4 Bobby... I heard the same, looks to me like those Texicans ain't on board with the program!"

"Word outta Dixie is all the big roads and most of the smaller asphalts leading into and outta the Lone Star are closed."

"Don't mess with Texas!"

"That's a 4 Bulldog... word is they declared independence."

With that, air horns began blasting their approval from every truck that was listening.

"I guess we got us a big audience there Double R"

"That's affirm... every big wheeler is eavesdropping piled up at the choke n puke's listening to the news... maybe I'll change my handle to concrete Cronkite."

"Ok there double C... you keep spreadin the word and I'll catch you on the flip flop."

"Roger that Ranger, Bulldog Bob OUT."

Tommy Gun Riley turned off the CB and turned to Jill. "Ever been to Texas?"

Don't dwell on what went wrong. Instead, focus on what to do next. Spend your energies on moving forward toward finding the answer.

Denis Waitley

Traveling south on I-55 toward St. Louis, Dennis Coleman settled in for the long drive that he had hoped he would never have to make to Arkansas. Mapping the route in his mind he gauged the time and distance at about 850 miles, between 16 and 17 hours.

He thought that the traffic seemed unusually light, not too many trucks on the road, but there were quite a few state troopers out. Just north of Springfield he had passed a small convoy of military troop carriers going the other way headed north.

Keeping his speed at around 70, Dennis figured that he wouldn't draw much attention from any Illinois state troopers that would pull him over and search his truck, but just in case he rehearsed his story over and over in his mind. It was a simple story, and really not that far from the truth. He was heading down to Arkansas for a camping and fishing trip with some friends. So as not to draw suspicion, he would show them the false bottom in the truck bed that he had used to hide the weapons, but now had only his outdoor gear hidden from any prying eyes that might steal it.

Just outside of St. Louis, he needed a break after 250 miles of going over and over the details of his mission in his mind. Also, unless you really enjoy looking at corn fields, southern Illinois scenery is pretty boring!

Pouring himself a cup of coffee from the thermos, his thoughts drifted back to the old man at the truck stop. He had only seen him for a few seconds, but it seemed as if the lines in his face instantly revealed something about his life and character, it showed a certain knowledge that one only gains through the good and the bad experiences during a life of struggle. But what struck Dennis the most was the look in the old man's eyes, a look of sadness, but also of an inner strength, a determination and resolve. *What was he thinking about as he stared out that window?* He wondered.

Dennis contemplated the old man for some time. He didn't think he was that perceptive, but there was something that made him instantly recognize all that in just those few short seconds. *Did the old man also see something in my face that prompted him to nod his head to me? Does my face reveal those same admirable characteristics? I hope so! Am I up to the task, or will I be found lacking?* Did other men also feel the same inner doubts when faced with a responsibility to discharge their duty? Not that he compared himself with great men such as Washington and Jefferson to Patton and MacArthur, but they too must have had the same misgivings as those of the ordinary soldiers who fought in every conflict from the American Revolution though Iraq and Afghanistan.

Approaching Memphis, Dennis's concentration was broken by the sight of the flashing lights of Tennessee state police cruisers about a mile ahead. Easing his foot from the accelerator, as his speed began to slow but his heart started to race, *was it a roadblock or just a random speeder?* Once closer he could see that it was a minor accident scene, one trooper was in the road directing traffic while another was assisting the driver of one of the cars. The trooper waved Dennis though and he resumed his speed.

Dennis's heart rate now began to return to normal and he returned to his thoughts. *"Now what was I thinking about?"* he said to himself, *"Soldiers!"* *The Civil War must have been the worst,* he thought, *the horrors of war but also the inner conflict of friend vs. friend, family vs. family...is that what this will come to? Brother against brother? Was it avoidable, or inevitable? What is the choice, to submit or resist? For years we talked about this, foretold that it would happen, we talked boldly about how we would resist, planned our strategy. But now that the time is upon us, will we prove to be true to our convictions, or did we just talk a good game?*

The thoughts kept coming while the hours and the miles fell behind. Now on I-40 west just outside of Little Rock, Dennis knew he would soon be looking for the I-30 west interchange to Hot Springs and through the Ouachita mountains to his final destination in Hatfield.

Dennis was tired...tired of driving, tired of thinking, but most of all tired of questioning himself! He was getting hungry, he needed food and he needed sleep, but he also needed something more, but what? Maybe he just needed to clear his head of everything and listen to some music. He reached into his pile of CDs, pulled out a Frank Sinatra, and shoved it into the player as "My Way" began to play.

"And now the end is near…"

Laughing to himself, *that's appropriate*, he thought. *But was it really the end?* Dennis checked his rear view mirror only to see the dark past left behind. Turning back to the black ribbon of asphalt road ahead, his headlights illuminated the promise of the future that lay before him.

Dennis returned to carefully listening to the lyrics.

Who hasn't had some regrets, he thought. *But he had always planned carefully in anything and did what he had to do without any apologies. Had he bitten off more than he could chew?* Immediately it came to him, the answer was no! *He had taken on many tough projects in his life and career with confidence and had always succeeded.*

Gaining some perspective, again he returned to the words of Ole Blue Eyes. *Dennis had done more than his share of laughing and crying, and he had even more than his share of women but he had never really loved any of them.*

A tear began to form as Dennis thoughtfully considered the final words, and now he felt a renewed sense of purpose and resolve, a comforting calm, followed by a surge of adrenaline. He realized what it was that he needed. Inspiration! It was more than this. It was far bigger than him or any one man. It would be a sacrifice for the greater good, not unlike our founding fathers. Dennis's attention returned to the road, a sign ahead read, Hatfield 10 miles.

"Thanks Frank. I needed that!"

In order to become the master, the politician poses as the servant.

Charles de Gaulle

"Well Meyer, what can we do?"

"Sir, your political options are very limited. You can justify the use force to quell insurrection in the cities as restoring order. However, the use of force to halt an entire state from rebellion will be seen as tyrannical, and possibly encourage other states that have active separatist movements such as Arizona, Louisiana and New Mexico to follow suit to come to its defense."

"And if I do nothing?" Brown deadpanned.

"If there are no consequences, this will also be seen as encouragement for those states, as well as a few others, to consider secession from the union," Epstein replied.

"What economic sanctions can we use?"

Epstein just shook his head. "Texas produces cattle, hogs, chickens eggs and dairy products, as well as a thriving fishing industry. Major crops are cotton, corn, grain, fruits and vegetables. It also produces peanuts and sugar cane. They lead the states in the total value of its mined products, producing large quantities of oil and natural gas." As if he were reading it from a page, Epstein continued. "It is responsible for about 1/5 of the country's oil production and almost 1/3 of the nation's supply of natural gas. Texas ranks first in the manufacturing of computers and electronic equipment; computers, electronic components, and military communication systems. Texas also leads the states in the manufacture of chemicals producing benzene, ethylene, fertilizers, propylene and sulfuric acid."

Brown just stared at Epstein as if he could not believe what he was being told.

"In conclusion Mr. President, Texas can sustain itself indefinitely. And since they would control approximately 1,800 miles of border along the Rio Grande, what materials they do not possess or produce, they could get in trade with a country such as Mexico, who would gladly purchase the oil and natural gas that they would no longer provide to us! In short, we are more dependent on them than they are on us."

"Couldn't we impose trade embargo sanctions on Mexico?"

With more than a hint of sarcasm in his voice, Epstein replied

"With general elections only a year away that should play well with the Latino community!"

Brown was becoming angry. He didn't like Meyer's tone, but like it or not, he knew that he would tell him the facts. "You're not leaving me much room to maneuver Meyer."

"You left yourself with no room Sir. Damned if you do, damned if you don't!" replied Epstein.

Brown returned the sarcasm. "So what you're telling me is that it's a shit sandwich, and I should try to bite off the piece with the least amount of turd, is that correct?"

Epstein's eyes narrowed. He had advised this man into the presidency. Now he had put himself in an untenable situation, and he expects me to pull a solution out of my ass!

Meyer Epstein straightened up as if coming to attention. "Yes Sir… Mr. President, SIR, you are screwed either way!"

Brown knew that Meyer's temper was legendary, he was known to use threats and profanity with members of the media and staff, and he knew that he had hit a nerve. He realized he needed to diffuse the situation.

"Then it would seem that military force is the option with the least amount of drawbacks, would you agree?"

"I would. But I must tell you that by doing so, you would basically be repeating history by, for the most part, FIRING ON FORT SUMPTER, and possibly igniting a second Civil War!"

Touching a finger to his temple as if in profound thought, Brown pondered that for a few moments before replying.

"Well, I've always wanted to be compared with Lincoln. Set up a meeting with General Crain."

CHAPTER FIVE

Texas has yet to learn submission to any oppression, come from what source it may.

Sam Houston

OUTSIDE OF THE GOVERNOR'S OFFICE, JOE SCOTT and Bill Baker waited patiently to be admitted for the morning briefing. For all that had transpired since yesterday, it seemed to be very quiet in the outer office. Barbara Rae, Walters's personal secretary, was busy fielding phone calls and taking messages.

Having only met him once, Scott did not know Jim Walter very well, so he was a little apprehensive as to how he should address him and how to present his strategy. He had heard from others that knew him well that he was a very down to earth, personable and friendly man, but this was not an ordinary situation. Should he be personal or strictly professional?

"You may go in now. Would you gentlemen like some coffee?" Rae asked.

Answering for himself and Baker, Scott replied. "Yes, black please… thank you."

The two men walked toward the large double doors of the governor's office.

"Well Bill, here we go." Scott's apprehensiveness quickly disappeared when he was met with the sight of Jim Walter talking on the phone with his feet up as he sat behind a large desk. Waving at them to have a seat, Walter put his hand over the mouth piece of the phone and mouthed "Be right with you."

Looking around Scott was immediately impressed by the warm atmosphere of the governor's office. Behind him to his left was a large Texas flag, and to his right was an empty space where an American flag once stood. The walls were not lined with the usual pictures of a politician shaking hands with celebrities or official accomplishments, but photos of him with his wife and children, of hunting and fishing trips with family and friends. Hanging in a prominent position was a portrait of John Wayne from the movie "The Shootist." Along the wall to the right was a bookshelf with books about the American Revolution, The Federalist Papers, the history of the Civil War, military histories of World War One and Two, Korea and Viet Nam, as well as biographies of Thomas Jefferson, George S. Patton, Douglas McArthur, Winston Churchill, and a complete collection of hard cover Louis L'Amour westerns and political novels by Tom Clancy.

"Ok Bob, you take care and say hello to Debbie. Talk to ya later." Walter hung up the phone and extending his hand he came around the desk.

"Joe, Bill good to see you!"

Taking his hand, Scott was surprised by the firmness of the grip of the handshake. "It's good to see you too sir," Scott replied.

Walter gestured toward the couch and some easy chairs. "Have a seat guys. Ron Thompson will be joining us but he has been delayed, so let's take the time to get acquainted while we're waiting for him."

At that moment, Barbara entered with a tray of coffee and breakfast rolls and laid it on the coffee table in the center. Gathering around the couch and chairs, Scott and Baker stood waiting for Walter to sit down first.

"Sit down fellas, have some coffee." Walter filled a cup and handed it to Scott and then filled another handing it to Baker before filling his own. Pushing the tray across the table, he asked "cream and sugar?"

"No thank you sir" Scott replied.

"OK, first of all let's knock off the sir bullshit, my name is Jim and you are Joe and Bill, got it?"

"Yes sir"

Walter just smirked and gave him a sideways glance. Picking up the tray he held it out offered them their choice.

"Here Bill, try an apple fritter, just save me a bear claw"

"Thank you Sss… Baker caught himself.

Smiling, Jim Walter offered the tray to Scott. "Joe. How is your wife Linda? Please send her my best."

"Just fine, I will and thank you for asking."

"And your son George, I hear he has a chance to start at tailback for the Longhorns next season! You must be very proud."

"Yes, we are."

Walter continued, "And Bill, I was happy to hear your wife is feeling better after her surgery. I had my wife Grace send her a bouquet of flowers. I understand she is partial to Texas Bluebonnets."

"Yes, she is, thanks Jim, I'm sure she will appreciate it."

Joe Scott was amazed. Here was the Governor, who was now the acting President of the Republic of Texas, a man who was now leading a rebellion, who must have been under tremendous pressure, and he seemed so relaxed. He had put them so at ease, serving coffee and pastries, refusing to be formally addressed, wanting to be called by his first name and addressing them by theirs. He had certainly done his homework, knowing the names of their wives and children; Scott would not have been surprised if he knew that his wedding anniversary was next week!

Sitting back in the lounge chair, Walter put his feet up on the coffee table took a bite of the bear claw and sipped his coffee. "So what do you think guys, be honest with me. Do you have any reservations about what we're doing?"

Looking toward Bill, Joe replied, "Bill and I are both Texas born and raised so I think I can speak for both of us when I say I don't think we had much choice Jim!" The President has basically torn up the Constitution and Bill of Rights, and us Texans won't stand for that. I believe that we are following the instructions of the Declaration of Independence and replacing a government that ignores the will of the people to such degree that it has lost its moral authority and has become too corrupt to effectively govern." Baker nodded in agreement.

Without saying a word, Walter reached across the table and extended his hand, shaking first with Joe and then Bill. Sitting back and sipping his coffee, Jim Walter paused before replying with a sigh,

"I could not have said it any better! Joe, you have no idea how glad I am to hear you say that, I feel it is of utmost importance that a commander is confident in his general's belief that his cause is just! If he does not process that conviction, he cannot effectively direct the troops under his command to carry out their orders."

A quiet fell over the room as all three men pondered what had just been said. Before Scott could respond, the silence was broken by the entrance of Ron Thompson.

Walter greeted Thomson. "Morning Ron, have some coffee."

"Good morning Jim." Thompson filled a cup and looked at the plate of pastries.

"Just once, couldn't you let me have the damn bear claw?" he said in an aggrieved tone.

"Quit your bitching and have a Danish," chuckled Walter.

"Ron, this is General Scott and Colonel Baker."

Thompson shook Scott's and Baker's hands. "Joe, Bill, nice to meet you."

Taking a seat in the opposite chair, Ron Thompson sat across from the governor.

Jim Walter spoke first. "Ok fellas, let's get down to business! Joe, update me on the progress of our preparations."

"Well Sir, Jim, as you know, in anticipation of these events, these clandestine preparations have been ongoing for the last five years. With the use of our network of volunteer citizen militia that have been undergoing training over the course of this period, and the strategic use of loyal local law enforcement officers and the Texas Rangers and national guard units, we have taken control of all military installations, airports, railroads and seaports along the gulf coast. Using these same units from counties along the borders of Louisiana, Arkansas, Oklahoma and New Mexico, we have set up armed checkpoints on all major highways and secondary roads leading into and out of Texas. We have effectively been able to close the borders between Texas and those surrounding states."

Walter nodded his head in approval. "Continue."

"Anti-personnel obstacles, as well as mines, have been strategically placed along the entire border. Tank traps are in place and are supported by concealed artillery units and infantry squads at their rear."

Walter listened thoughtfully as Scott detailed his plans before asking, "Joe, since the military knows what our capabilities are, how would we defend and repel an attack from superior forces?"

Joe turned to Bill for the answer.

"Well Jim, in all honesty, we can't."

Thompson was stunned. "Colonel, we were led to believe that plans had been developed to defend Texas from any such assault, and now you're sitting here telling us that it can't be done!"

"Our plan, Mr. Thompson, is to by means of deception, diplomacy and public opinion, to discourage any attack," replied Bill calmly.

Sitting forward in his chair, and before Thompson could question Baker further, Walter raised his hand to stop him. "Please explain Bill."

"For the last five years, under the guise of dummy corporations set up as joint ventures between government and private companies using public and private funds to acquire agricultural equipment, we have been secretly purchasing surplus Soviet T-64, T-72 and T-80 battle tanks through third world countries, and refitting them for our use to supplement our forces. We have also been diligent in employing expert modelers to manufacture exact copy shells of these tanks that are made from plywood and placed over automobiles as decoys, that are mixed in with the real Soviet and our existing U.S. built armor. These mobile decoys will constantly be redeployed so as to give the illusion of ten times our known strength to any aerial reconnaissance, which will be unable to detect the difference."

"Go on," Walter said smiling.

Joe took over. "We have sympathetic members of the House and Senate that would draft a joint resolution advising the President and the DOD that any attack would be met with such resistance of the civilian population, similar to the logic behind not invading Japan, that an attack would be met with an armed Texan behind every blade of grass and oppose any military action being taken. This would be covered by C-Span, which we hope would sway popular opinion of a war-weary America to a non-aggressive use of diplomacy to avoid such a catastrophe."

Walter thoughtfully considered what he had just been told. *What would he do if he were in Brown's position? Faced with these two equally bad choices would put him in a very unenviable political position.*

"Ok guys. I'm President Brown. I'm in my second term so I really don't care about the polls or my approval rating at this point. On the one hand, I do nothing, and risk further disintegration of the union. On the other hand, I take decisive military action. Knowing this President, I go with option B! Now what?"

"We know that President Brown's closest military advisor is chairman of the Joint Chiefs of Staff General George Crain. General Scott knows Crain, and knows his tactics," Baker replied.

Joe interrupted. "George and I went to the Point together, Jim. He and I spent countless hours playing a game called Stratego, where the ultimate objective was to capture the enemy's flag. He is a by-the-book tactician; he will carefully assess his Intel, and look to exploit the weak point nearest his strategic initiative, which would be to capture Austin."

"So how do you propose to prevent this?" Thompson asked.

Taking out a map, Bill spread it across the coffee table, as Joe continued to outline his plan.

"Operation Soft Spot is designed to provide the enemy with what would appear to be a weak area of defense along the Louisiana border north of I-10 east of Beaumont, in an area of terrain that would support the use of heavy armor with the shortest distance approximately 250 miles to the objective-Austin. Our goal is to induce an attack through this narrow corridor, offering a token resistance, and fall back to a position behind a series of Howitzer artillery batteries deployed approximately one to two miles to the rear."

Pointing to a spot on the map, he continued. "Once the enemy advances to this position, a coordinated counter-attack would be launched that calls for the Howitzers to open fire and take out the Neches River Bridge to the rear, preventing the enemy's retreat. The M-105's would then open fire on their position, forcing them to scatter their forces to the north and the south, where they will be met on both flanks by our M-1

Abrams armored brigades supported by units of Texas Guard infantry. Apache attack helicopters will then strafe the enemy column with rocket fire while the eastern-most infantry units with aerial support by the Apaches will then employ a pincer movement, advancing to a position at the enemy's rear, effectively boxing them in and cutting off their escape route and supply lines. This would force the field commander to choose between a humiliating surrender, or a disastrous defeat!"

Tilting his head backward, as if in deep thought, Jim Walter closed his eyes and sat back in his chair. After a few silent moments, without opening his eyes, Walter asked

"And what contingency plans are there if Crain does not do as you anticipated or this defense fails?"

"Plan B," answered Joe.

"And what is plan B?"

"Operation Punt calls for the relocation of the Texas government to the buildings surrounding the Alamo in San Antonio, retreating and marshalling of all our remaining forces as a last line of defense."

Walters's eyes popped open "You're kidding?"

"No Sir… in this scenario, our hope is that the symbolism of such a move would generate the needed surge of public opinion in our favor to halt any continued advance!" Joe replied.

Walter looked at Thompson. "Any more thoughts or questions Ron?" Thompson shook his head no. Standing, he said "Well gentlemen that was a very detailed and concise report."

Thompson, Scott and Baker stood, as they all shook hands and made their goodbyes.

Upon reaching the door, Scott heard Walter call to him. "Oh, Joe."

Turning to face Jim Walter, Joe replied "Yes Jim?"

"I hope you and Linda have a happy anniversary next week!"

"Thanks Jim, I hope so too."

Stepping through the large double doors, Joe thought "Well I'll be a son of a bitch!"

True patriotism hates injustice in its own land more than anywhere else.

Clarence Darrow

Sitting at his kitchen table, Tommy "Gun" Riley pondered the long drive to Texas… *it's close to a thousand miles,* he thought, *how long would it take, a day, a day and a half? Maybe more if we have to use back roads.*

Tommy didn't want to leave but he knew he couldn't stay and live in a country that no longer allowed its people the cornerstone of all freedom, the right to bear arms! He watched as this President had slowly eroded the Bill of Rights by spying on the press, effectively silencing his critics by destroying the first amendment and the people's right to know, then by using the IRS to intimidate political groups that opposed his socialist agenda, and now using his power to remove the second amendment to prevent the people from resisting.

"Dad," Jill called from her bedroom, "can I bring the photo albums?"

Tommy did not answer; he was lost in thought about what they would need to pack, not only for the long trip, but for a quick permanent move. He reasoned that they would be able to acquire weapons and ammunition in Texas, so they should bury them in the storm shelter.

Walking into the kitchen, Jill raised her normally soft voice and loudly called out again, "DAD!"

With a questioning look, Tommy turned to look at Jill.

Holding up the albums stuffed with pictures of family history "Photos?" she asked.

"Sure honey."

Returning to her room, Jill finished packing her belongings, before moving to her father's room to pack up his. Retrieving the large suitcase from the closet, Jill began going through the dresser drawers; T- shirts, socks, underwear, moving to the closet she grabbed a few pairs of pants and shirts and carefully folded them and placed them into the case. Looking into the closet once more to see if she had forgotten anything, she reached for an old camouflage jacket on the upper shelf. Pulling it down, she noticed a fairly large box behind it. Taking the box down, she carefully laid it on the bed and opened it. Inside the box were all her father's medals, ribbons and other decorations he had earned during his military career. Tommy "Gun" Riley was not the kind of man that talked about his combat experiences; Jill knew that her father was a war hero, but she was shocked by what was in the box, Two Purple Hearts, two Silver Stars, and a Navy Cross. Another box lay underneath. Opening it, her eyes widened when she saw a light blue ribbon with stars with the word VALOR on it...the Medal of Honor. Jill was filled with a sense of pride that her father had done so much for the country he loved, but was also saddened that he felt so betrayed by the government he had so faithfully served that he felt he now had to leave it. As delicately as if she were handling eggs, Jill placed the medals back into the box, wrapped it in the jacket and placed it in the suitcase. *This is coming with us!*

Freedom is the sure possession of those alone who have the courage to defend it.

Pericles

Sitting across the table from the old man, Dennis Coleman saw a tear roll down his cheek, and then the waitress came and took a seat next to him. Looking at the old man and then at him, she took both of their hands and looked at Dennis and smiled. A pain shot though his side, but he returned the smile. Another, sharper, pain hit Dennis in the ribs. His eyes opened to see a man standing above him.

"Are you Coleman?"

Dennis quickly studied the man hovering over him. The quintessential country man; 35 to 40 years old, neck-length brown hair, beard and mustache, tall-about six feet, 190 lbs. give or take, his broad shoulders and muscled arms gave away what must have been a life spent doing physical labor. He wore worn blue denim jeans, a John Deere T-shirt, work boots and a Ford ball cap. *The man was a walking cliché!* Dennis nodded.

"Did you get much sleep?"

"A few hours I guess, what time is it?"

Smiling, the man replied "breakfast time. Name's Charley, Charley Pine."

Standing, he extended his right hand. "Dennis Coleman."

Charley took Dennis's hand in a firm grip and shook it. "Glad to know ya. Miguel called and said you were on your way, you hungry?"

"Starving!"

"Well come on then. We're camped about a quarter mile down that trail," he said, pointing to what looked like an animal trail through the trees leading off to the west.

Grabbing a roll of toilet paper from his pack, Dennis walked toward the woods. Without looking back, Dennis replied

"Ok, I'll be there in a few minutes; I gotta take care of business."

Later, walking down the trail, his nose picked up the scent of coffee and bacon. After another 30 or 40 yards he came to a clearing where he found their camp next to a small stream. Charley and another man were sitting around a small fire drinking hot coffee and frying bacon.

"Have a seat," Charley said. "Dennis, this here's Jack." Without saying a word, Jack stood and shook Coleman's hand and went back to tending the bacon. Charley handed Coleman a steaming cup of coffee "Long ride huh?"

"Yeah." Taking the cup and holding it up to his nose, he said "Thanks." Dennis thought of the aroma of the coffee the waitress brought to him yesterday, he tried to recall her voice. *Why did he dream of her and the old man?* Taking a small sip and then a gulp and then another, he drained the cup and handed it back to Charley.

"Want another?"

"Please."

Charley filled the cup again and handed it back to Coleman. This time, Dennis savored the taste, coffee brewed over an open camp fire has a different flavor to it, a taste of the open air and fire, and it was strong, just the way he liked it. Lighting a smoke, he took a long drag and inhaled, his thoughts again going back to the dream. *What could it have meant? What do the woman and old man have in common? What was her name?* Reaching into his jacket pocket his fingers felt for the check stub, pulling it out, he read Jill.

A nudge on his leg brought him back to reality.

"Eat," said Jack handing him a plate with bacon and a slice of toasted bread loaded with bacon fat and ketchup.

Dennis put the stub back into his pocket and took the plate from Jack. "Thank you," he said. Dennis's memories went back to when his grandfather would make him bacon fat and ketchup sandwiches, and tell him stories of the hard times when he was a boy and what people would do to stretch the dollar; apparently it survived the test of time from then until now. *What goes around comes around,* he thought.

"Eat up; we got a long day ahead. We got a two hour ride and a long walk into those hills," Charley said, pointing toward the Ouachita Mountains. Dennis finished his breakfast and got up to help Charley and Jack, who had already begun to pack up camp. His thoughts again returned to the blonde haired waitress with the pretty smile. *I hope I meet her again.*

CHAPTER SIX

A fanatic is one who can't change his mind and won't change the subject.

Winston Churchill

OUTSIDE THE OVAL OFFICE, GENERAL GEORGE Crain waited impatiently to be admitted. He was a man that did not like to be kept waiting, but he was also a man with ambitions beyond chairman of the Joint Chiefs of Staff. *Could this be his moment,* he thought, like Washington, Grant and Eisenhower before him, *could this be the opportunity that leads him to the Presidency?* He must proceed with caution or it could also spell the end of a brilliant military career!

"You may go in now General."

Briefcase in hand, Crain rose and approached the door to the Oval Office. Pausing momentarily, he opened the door and

Jim Dulski

entered. Seated behind the resolute desk sat President Brown, with his chief of staff Meyer Epstein seated in a chair in front.

"Mr. President, Meyer." Shaking their hands, Crain sat next to Epstein.

"Well George, give me some good news. What have you got for us?" Brown asked.

"Sir, I'm afraid I don't have much good news for you." Reaching into his briefcase, Crain removed a file folder containing aerial photography of Texas's defenses. Handing a photo to Brown, he continued.

"As you can see by these photographs and the latest Intel, this is not intended to be a symbolic gesture by Texas, they definitely mean business. They have constructed defensive positions along all the major and secondary roads."

Glaring at Crain, Brown momentarily glanced at the photo before passing it on to Epstein. "Continue General," Brown said.

"It would appear that they have been preparing for this for some time."

"What gives you that indication?" Brown asked.

"The swiftness, timing, and precision of the operations, employed to overrun every military installation in the state, as well as their ability to control all land, air, and sea ports of entry, and choke off all primary and secondary roads indicates a high level of cooperation between state government, military, law enforcement, civilian and private companies, and that these preparations have been preplanned and ongoing for a number of years."

"How many years do you think this has been going on?" Brown asked.

"Sir, at least five to six years would be required to prepare such a coordinated effort."

"So that would mean that these preparations would have had to begin almost precisely from the time our administration took office, is that correct?"

"It would appear that way sir," Crain replied.

As if seeking validation, Brown turned his gaze to Epstein, whose only response was to shrug his shoulders as if to say, *what did you expect?* Brown returned to Crain.

"General, how is it possible that this could have gone undetected for all this time?"

"We are not in the business of accessing the military strength and capabilities, or investigating possible conspiracy theories regarding individual states sir. Might I suggest you ask the Director of the FBI that question?" Crain replied in a slightly sarcastic tone.

Since the FBI director was a close personal friend of the President, and not well liked by the staff, Brown didn't like that answer, and a slight smirk crossed Epstein's face. Brown was becoming irritated and his face was beginning to show the mounting tension. Publically he was thought to be cool, always giving the impression that he was the smartest guy in the room and always in control, but privately he was known for his emotional outbursts that revealed his arrogance. He knew Crain had ambitions and saw an opportunity, so he must control his emotions in this situation.

Pausing for a moment, and with the slightest bit of sarcasm Brown asked "Anything else... GENERAL?"

"Yes sir. The strength of their forces far exceeds our expectations. Aerial reconnaissance reveals that they have ten times more armor than last inventoried."

For the first time, Brown's face showed surprise.

Crain continued. "It seems that along with the standard U.S. military armored vehicles, of which they have far more than anticipated, they have somehow acquired hundreds of Soviet T-64, T-72 and T-80 battle tanks."

Slamming his clenched fist on the desktop, Brown screamed "How is that possible?"

Epstein already knew the answer and he could hardly contain himself.

"That, sir, is a question for the director of the CIA." This was another of Brown's cronies that was given the job by recess appointment.

Brown was now absolutely livid.

"And how do you plan to quell this rebellion General?" he yelled.

"My staff is in the process of evaluating the Intel so we can identify a weakness that can be exploited. From what we now know, General Joe Scott is in charge of their forces."

"What do we know about him?" Brown questioned.

Again reaching into his briefcase, Crain produced Scott's dossier and handed it to Brown. "Joe and I attended West Point together. He is an excellent tactician and experienced field commander. We know each other well and I can predict his moves as well as he can predict mine. However, as well as they are equipped, he is out-manned and out-gunned and he knows it, so I am sure that he will attempt a diversion of some sort to draw our forces into a trap."

Brown sat back in his chair and folded his hands in front of his face. "How soon can you have a plan, and how long will it take to implement it?"

"My staff should have plans ready in a few days with another two to three days to prepare and transport our forces."

"Very good, General. Is there anything else?"

"Yes sir… may I speak freely?"

"Go right ahead."

"Mr. President, I strongly advise you to pursue a political solution to this problem! Our troops will have mixed emotions about firing on U.S. citizens, and we can expect a number of soldiers to go AWOL, refuse to follow orders to fire, and some will also join Texas's cause." Brown nodded his head in understanding as Crain continued.

"If it comes down to actual armed conflict, our forces will no doubt overwhelm them. However, we will not only be up against their military and law enforcement, but you can be assured that a very large number of civilians will take part in the battle. Casualties on both sides will be to such a high degree that it will make Gettysburg seem like a garden party!"

Again Brown nodded. "Rest assured, General, your concerns will be taken into account; in the meantime make whatever preparations that are necessary to put an end to this rebellion."

Standing to leave, Crain replied "Yes sir," and walked toward the door. Once outside, he noticed a number of people waiting to see the President, including the attorney general and members of the armed services committee, as well as the Secretary of Defense and the ambassador to the United Nations. Crain *wondered what they could be meeting about?*

CHAPTER SEVEN

Suppose you were an idiot, and suppose you were a member of Congress; but I repeat myself.

Mark Twain

THE GAVEL CAME DOWN HARD. "THE HOUSE WILL come to order!" bellowed Speaker of the House John Rainer. "The Chair recognizes the representative from the state of Texas"

Rising to speak, Congressman David Johnson stood to address the members of the House.

"Point of order," came a loud voice from across the aisle. "Mr. Speaker, I object, since the state of Texas has seceded from the union, this man no longer has a voice in this chamber," said the representative from California, minority leader Stacy

Pulazi. "I therefore move that the gentleman be expelled from this body."

Raising his hand, New York Representative Harley Stengel declared, "I second the motion!"

"The question of the expulsion of the gentleman from Texas is now open for debate," said Rainer.

Standing to speak, Florida Representative Betty Goldman Schmidt shouted, "Mr. Speaker!"

"The Chair recognizes the gentle lady from Florida."

"Mr. Chairman, the gentleman from Texas should not be allowed to address this body, as the state which he represents has engaged in conspiracy, sedition and treason by seceding from the United States of America. She continued, "He has violated his oath of office to preserve, protect and defend the constitution."

"Mathew Krys with NSMBA in New York, Craig, tell us what is happening on the floor."

"Thank you Mathew. This is Craig Stephens reporting from Washington, where debate has begun to expel the Texas delegation from the chamber. Speaker Rainer has just closed the floor to hear further debate, let's listen in."

"The chair again recognizes the gentleman from Texas. Mr. Johnson."

Reading from a prepared text, Congressman David Johnson began, "Mr. Speaker, I rise today to address this sacred chamber as a member for the last time. I must resign as a representative of this body in order to assume a greater calling. It is with great pride that I have accepted the position as ambassador of the Republic of Texas to the United States of America."

Yells of traitor and treason erupted from across the aisle and the gallery. Speaker Rainer banged down hard several times before order was restored. "WE WILL MAINTAIN ORDER," the Speaker admonished, "I REMIND THE GALLERY THAT THEY ARE OUR GUESTS AND WILL BEHAVE AS SUCH OR BE EJECTED FROM THE CHAMBER. THERE WILL BE NO FURTHER OUTBUSTS FROM THE FLOOR AND DECORUM WILL BE MAINTAINED!" He looked around the room. "Mr. Johnson, you may continue."

"Thank you Mr. Speaker. In my over twenty years of service representing the people of Texas as a member of this body, I have watched as we have become more and more divided; divided not only as a congress, but as a nation and a people! We have become so intent on advancing the agendas of our parties and special interests that the best interests of the nation or the people are no longer taken into consideration. We are no longer guided by what is right, but what is politically expedient!"

Pointing a finger across the aisle, he continued. "I have witnessed the corruption of our members by foreign interests, by Communists and Socialists whose intent is to destroy the fabric of our Republic." Turning to face his own colleagues, Johnson again pointed. "I have also witnessed the transformation of members of my own party from moderate to militant to the point of bordering on Fascism! I have watched as our leadership has failed to lead, has orchestrated a failed foreign policy designed to diminish our stature as the world's superpower, watched as nation after nation who once would not dare challenge our resolve to protect our interests or the interests of our allies, break treaties to acquire land or assume power and control over its neighbors; WATCHED as terrorists are traded for traitors and are set free to rejoin the battle; WATCHED while a United States Marine rots in a Mexican prison cell for making a wrong turn! Mr. Speaker, I have WATCHED as a multitude of illegal immigrants are allowed to cross our unsecured borders, WATCHED as our border security agents have been wounded and killed in the line of duty. WATCHED as the proliferation of gun trafficking across the border proceeded at a fast and furious pace, WATCHED as government agencies targeted our citizens for their political beliefs, WATCHED as they conspired to cover up the lack of security that lead to the assassination of our ambassador! WATCHED as the main stream media conspired to cover up scandal after scandal by its lack of coverage of these events, even after one its own journalists was filmed being beheaded and broadcast on social media! WATCHED as our leaders fan the flames of racism, class warfare and division to serve their political aims! MR. SPEAKER. As Abraham Lincoln once said, "A house divided against itself cannot stand!"

Three things cannot be long hidden: the sun, the moon, and the truth.

Buddha

Jill Riley could not remember ever feeling so safe and secure in any man's arms before. Her head against his chest, she could feel the beating of his heart. Looking up into his eyes, she could sense the sadness there, he leaned down and gently kissed her, pulling back he paused and looked directly into her eyes as If seeking her approval, he leaned in again and...

"This here is Tommy "Gun", southbound on double nickel, anyone got sports updates, come back." Jill awoke with a start, but did not open her eyes, pretending to still be sound asleep; she sat quietly listening to her father's CB conversation.

"Roger that, Gun, this here is Turbo Terry. Looks like you got smooth sailin south all the way to Saint Louie. Word is, north of Memphis they are stopping and searching anything south bound with Patriotic bumper stickers, American flags and the like and calling it a safety inspection."

Tommy Riley thought about that for a minute before responding, he didn't want to tag himself to anyone that might be listening in on the conversation.

"10-4 Turbo, I hear same thing going south from Louisville, Omaha, and KC." Tommy knew that with all the NRA and Marine Corp stickers on this truck he would be stopped for sure.

"That's a rodge Gun...you can get the news at just about any food–n-fuel stop and get the scuttle butt on the detour routes into Dixie."

Still not fully awake, Jill opened her eyes and looked out the window at the endless rows of corn fields "Dad, where are we" she asked.

"Just north of St. Louis, you should go back to sleep baby, cause we still have a long way to go." Jill wondered *why she would dream of the tall man she served breakfast to yesterday. This was so unlike her, it was one thing to give a man her phone number, but to have dreams of warm kisses and embraces like some young school girl was another.* Hell she thought, *what were the odds she would ever see him again? Even if she had stayed behind in Illinois, and now with all that had happened, and them on their way to Texas, it was a certainty that their paths would never cross again.*

The Clinton administration launched an attack on people in Texas because those people were religious nuts with guns. Hell, this country was founded by religious nuts with guns. Who does Bill Clinton think stepped ashore on Plymouth Rock?

P. J. O'Rourke

Stepping through the door of the Texas Senate chamber, the sergeant-at-arms bellowed, "Ladies and gentlemen, The President of the Republic of Texas."

Jim Walter walked slowly down the aisle to a smattering of applause from a somber delegation of 31 state senators and 150 representatives; shaking hands with several of whom were giving him support and words of encouragement, while a few others showed their disdain by turning their backs to him. Walker strode up to the podium. Waiting for the applause to subside, he motioned for everyone to be seated before he began.

"My fellow Texans today is an historic day, as profound as March 2nd, 1836 where at Washington on The Brazos, 59 of our citizens, including Sam Houston, signed our first Declaration of Independence from Mexico. History has since judged these actions. Today, 179 years later, we again gather to sign documents of Independence and a National Constitution.

Many of you are troubled by this action, as you well should be. However, many more have expressed that we have no alternative left but to secede from the union in order to remain a free people. Even though they will not be properly portrayed by the media to the rest of the world, let me again state our intentions. We, the citizens of The Republic of Texas, do not celebrate this action, nor do we wish for armed conflict with our brothers, neighbors and friends of the United States. We wish to be and remain a free people; free to make decisions to govern the course of our lives as we see fit, free to choose our health care according to our individual needs and resources, free to reap the benefits of our labors, and free to live in peace and prosper as a people to raise our families according to our most sacred beliefs and traditions.

However, let it be known, here, now and forever that the people of Texas shall never capitulate to a despotic form of government that seeks to have all power and complete control over the lives of its citizens! Let the word go forth that we offer our hand to the world in friendship, but if we are attacked, whether economically or militarily, we shall repel and defend in kind! Again, let history be the judge of our actions. God Bless the Republic of Texas, thank you."

With that, to a standing ovation, a saddened but serious Jim Walker looked straight ahead as he walked slowly from the podium, this time not stopping to shake hands as he made his way back up the aisle.

People who work together will win, whether it be against complex football defenses, or the problems of modern society.

Vince Lombardi

Dennis had been following Jack and Charley for three hours, hiking up higher into the foothills of the Ouachita Mountains. Stopping occasionally to look at strange markings on trees, they pushed on though the dense forest. Coming to a clearing, they came upon a small hanging valley which had a small stream running through it. Crossing the stream, Charley paused at an old stump about ten yards up the bank. Looking at his compass, he walked about 15 paces to the west and stopped at a large boulder surrounded by an assortment of smaller stones. Jack and Charley studied and discussed the arrangement of the stones for a while before they came to an agreement. Charley would work up the trail to the west, Jack would search the stream bank and he was to go back up the trail they came down about a mile or so to cover any sign that they had made coming up.

Dennis knew that they did not want him to witness the find, so he did as he was told and worked their back trail and covered sign. Returning to the stream about two hours later, he found that Jack had made camp and Charley already had a line in the water and two on the stringer. Dennis walked to where they had laid their gear under the trees above the bank to find

Jack along with a box that looked to be over a hundred years old that he was sitting on.

"That what we came for?"

"Yup," Jack replied.

"Not much for conversation, are ya."

With a sly grin, shaking his head again, Jack replied with a single word "Nope."

Just then, Charley came up the bank with five river cat on the string. Without saying a word Jack stood up and walked off into the woods, and Charley sat down on the box and began to skin the fish. *These two must have known each other since Moses wore short pants, because they seemed to instinctively know what the other was thinking and knew what each other would do.*

Tossing a pot at Dennis, Charley asked, "Coleman… you wanna get some water?"

Dennis walked down to the bank and upstream about ten yards before he drew about a gallon of fresh mountain water from the stream. Standing, he looked over the small valley. *This was a good place* he thought. It appeared that there was only one entrance to it and it looked to be completely untouched and unspoiled by campers or hikers. With the mountains rising on the western end, the forest guarding its entrance on the east, and the stream flowing from north to south it was a perfect place to hide something, for it was truly the definition of a hidden valley.

Walking back up to camp, Coleman handed the pot of water to Charley, who had finished skinning the catfish, and commenced to gather wood for a fire. Dennis figured he better get a fire going soon, as by the looks of the sun they only had about 2 hours of daylight left. He began building a small fire under the lower branches of the tree at the edge of the camp. Although he gathered only dry wood that wouldn't produce much smoke, this would help to filter the fire light. About that time, Jack reappeared from the forest with some kindling and saw the small fire that Dennis had made. Jack looked over to Charley, grinned and dropped his bundle of kindling before turning to give Dennis an approving nod of the head, and headed off to get water for coffee.

Fire, water, food, shelter, CHECK. Dennis set up his two man pup tent in about ten minutes, before finally settling down fireside to watch as Charley prepared the fish, the aroma of coffee filling the air. Dennis sat back and pondered the mission ahead, but his mind wandered back to Jill the waitress. Breathing clean air and hiking in the mountains, catching fresh fish and drinking hot coffee made with spring fed water from a stream in a beautiful hidden valley. *What a great camping trip this would be to enjoy with a good woman by his side!*

Returning to camp, Jack handed Dennis a plate of fried fish and some bread. "Eat," he said.

"Thanks." Dennis took the plate and set it down next to his feet. Standing, he refilled Jack and Charley's cups before pouring himself a fresh cup a Joe. The coffee was just how he liked it-steaming hot, strong and black. The three men ate in silence. When they had finished, Jack gathered up the plates, cups, and pan and took them to rinse in the stream.

Nighttime had now descended on the valley, and Dennis added some fuel to the fire. Sitting down, Jack pulled out a harmonica and began to play a slow blues tune. Dennis had to laugh to himself as he thought *this is a scene right out of Deliverance.*

Charley began to speak. "We'll get a goin' at first light. We'll make our way back using the other trail and..."

"What other trail?" Dennis asked.

Charley just smiled. He gestured over his right shoulder and said "that one over yonder."

Dennis looked past Charley at the forest. "I didn't see any trail," he said.

Jack stopped playing long enough to say, "It's there."

With more than a hint of sarcasm, Dennis replied, "Wow, Jack two whole words... don't wear yourself out!" Jack just grinned and returned to playing his Hohner.

Charley went on. "The signs say to follow the camel trail back down the mountain until we see the camels hump."

Camel trail? Don't ask, he thought. "What are we going back that way for?"

"To fetch us another box," Charley replied, as he patted the crate he was sitting on.

For the rest of the evening, Charley and Dennis sat in silence; drinking coffee and listening to Jack play his Hohner Blues Harp. After about an hour Dennis crawled into his tent and within minutes fell into a deep sleep.

CHAPTER EIGHT

Better to fight for something than live for nothing.

George S. Patton

THE ROOM WAS FILLED WITH THE CLATTER OF VOICES when a loud voice rose above the din. "Attention!" Major Bob Bricker called out as General Joe Scott entered the room to meet with the unit commanders. As Joe walked slowly to the front and center before pausing to salute the soldiers standing before him, he was reminded of the opening scene of *Patton*. He quietly surveyed the group of Texas Guard, Militia and law enforcement that made up the command structure of the Texas military. Looking left then right then left again, Scott stood silently for about 30 seconds before giving the order, "At ease gentlemen." Everyone stood at parade rest. Joe began.

"Be seated. You gentlemen are gathered here because you have volunteered to defend not only your country, but your homes, and the freedoms that belong to you and your children, your family and those of your neighbors, and their neighbors and their neighbor's neighbors. I know that many of you must be apprehensive and have reservations and mixed emotions about the mission ahead of us. HELL! You wouldn't be human if you didn't! But make no mistake gentlemen. Your cause is just and righteous! If it comes down to armed conflict between Texas and the United States, you will be engaged in battle with men who, until three days ago, wore the same uniform as you, Fellow Army, Marines, Navy and Air Force, men that you considered your brothers in arms."

Scott's voice now rose in volume. "But gentlemen, I say to you, here and now, that as of this moment you must dispel these thoughts, you must put aside your fears, just as those who fought against the British, or those that fought for the Union or the Confederacy had to do during the Revolutionary and Civil Wars before us!" Looking into the faces of the soldiers seated before him, he could see that they were transfixed and hanging on every word. Pacing back and forth for dramatic effect, and pointing out to nobody in particular, Scott felt like a rock star that was in the zone!

"We have planned for, and have arrived at, this moment in history, knowing that this is our destiny!" Scott's voice now grew even louder. "WE MUST DO OUR DUTY! WE MUST NOT FAIL, AND WE SHALL PREVAIL!" Joe Scott again paused and looked around the room, "Now…you men have your orders. DISMISSED!"

"ATTENTION!" Bricker again called out. With that, the room rose to its feet and General Joseph Jackson Scott turned and left the room.

The military don't start wars. Politicians start wars.

William Westmoreland

"Roger that base…approaching target area…OVER." Flying east along the Oklahoma-Texas border, turning the Lockheed Martin F-22 Raptor to the south, Air Force Captain John Michaels adjusted his 6 foot 3 inch, 220 pound frame in his seat. Michaels was rather large for a pilot, which earned him the call sign "Eclipse," because he blocked a lot of sunlight. Increasing his altitude to angels 12, Michaels began his run into Texas air space. His mission was to photograph military defensive positions and gauge the Texas Air Corps response to an intrusion by a foreign aircraft entering its air space. "Have entered enemy airspace…OVER." At that moment his panel lit up, he was being tracked.

"Attention unidentified aircraft, you have entered Texas national airspace…this is restricted airspace…please identify yourself and state your business or be fired upon…OVER."

At that moment, 4 bogies appeared on Michaels radar screen, approaching his position at high speed from the west. "Eclipse to base…I am being tracked by enemy radar…have 4 bogies approaching my position at 10,000 angels from west at Mach 1.5, what are my rules of engagement… OVER?"

"10-4 Eclipse, continue your run to target, if engaged take evasive action. DO NOT, I REPEAT, DO NOT TAKE HOSTILE ACTION! OVER." *And what am I supposed to do if I'm fired upon?* Michaels thought to himself. "Roger that base, Eclipse is 8 minutes to target, OVER." Just then four F/A – 18 Super Hornets took positions at 12 and 6 o'clock off each wing.

"ATTENTION U.S. AIRCRAFT." Looking over his left shoulder the young pilot saluted Michaels. "This is Texas Air Guard escort flight leader Captain Joe Glipski, OVER."

Returning the salute Michaels replied, "Hello Joe… Captain John "Eclipse" Michaels, United States Air Force here, nice day for flying wouldn't you say? OVER."

"Yes sir it is a beautiful day for flying, OVER." Glipski replied in his thick southern drawl

"So Captain, what can I do for you and the Texas Air Guard on this fine day? OVER?"

Laughing, Glipski replied, "You can call me Ramrod. Sir, my orders are to escort you out of Texas airspace. OVER."

Laughing, Eclipse replied "But I haven't seen all of Texas yet, OVER."

"Well sir normally we enjoy entertaining out-of-state guests with our fine southern hospitality, but in this case I'm pretty sure that they don't want you to see all of Texas at this time. OVER."

Again laughing "I think we can be fairly certain you're right about that Ramrod. Ramrod, huh, should I ask? OVER."

"Long story… no pun intended. OVER."

Eclipse nodded. "And what if I do not comply? OVER."

"In that case, my orders are then to force you to the ground by whatever means necessary. And as you said Captain, it's a beautiful day for flying; please don't ruin it by making me carry out that order! OVER."

With that Captain John Michaels saluted, rolled right, and began evasive tactics. With the F/A-18's falling into attack formation, and even though the Raptor was a far superior plane, it would not be able to long out-maneuver a disadvantage of 4 to 1.

"Eclipse to base five minutes to target… am being engaged by four … repeat four hostile aircraft, OVER."

"Roger Eclipse… if fired upon you may return fire at your discretion, OVER."

Glancing quickly over both shoulders, he could see that he was boxed in. Ramrod had taken up perfect firing position directly behind him, and just at that moment he let loose with a five second burst from his 20MM cannon. Eclipse rolled left, then banked right to evade fire, but he knew that from that position he could not miss unless it was on purpose. It was just a warning shot!

"Eclipse to base, four minutes to target have been fired upon have taken evasive maneuvers but am totally defensive, OVER."

"10-4 continue evasive and proceed to target, OVER."

At that point the 6 o'clock bogie dropped out, leaving an opening in the box for him to escape. Eclipse decreased altitude and air speed but continued on course to target. Another cannon burst caused him to bank right and left to return to course. Again he knew that it was an intentional miss.

Three minutes to target. Two more bursts were followed by "Ramrod to Eclipse...please Captain, let us escort you out of Texas airspace, OVER!"

Two minutes to target. "Eclipse to Ramrod...I have my orders, as do you. You're a good man Joe; NOW CARRY OUT YOUR ORDERS CAPTAIN! Eclipse over and out."

One minute to target. A shrill warning alarm alerted Eclipse that he had been missile locked. 30 seconds…doors open, camera on.

Wiping tears away from his face, Captain Joe Glipski radioed his group. "Ramrod to escort flight, this is my call. FOX 1 missile away." The AIM 9 sidewinder streaked toward Eclipse, who banked left and somehow miraculously evaded it, but it brought Eclipse right into his cannon sights. Ramrod let loose a five second burst, then paused and followed with another burst of ten seconds. The second burst scored a hit, taking out one of the Raptor's Pratt & Whitney engines, and part of its right wing.

"Eclipse to base, Mayday, am hit, and going down!"

Watching the Raptor tumble toward earth, Glipski searched the sky for a parachute. *Come on John, get out of there. Please God, get him out of there, he prayed.* Finally, after what seemed like an eternity, the canopy of Eclipse's parachute appeared. "Ramrod to base…target is destroyed, pilot ejected…alert rescue, OVER."

"Roger that Ramrod…base out."

"Ramrod to escort flight… return to base, OVER AND OUT."

Absolute truth is a very rare and dangerous commodity in the context of professional journalism.

Hunter S. Thompson

After fueling up and getting supplies from the Stop-N-Go, Tommy Gun pulled out his map to find an alternate route around Memphis. "Break one nine…Tommy Gun lookin for smoky report from north bound 40/240, anyone out there got a current news report?" Sitting there waiting for a reply, Tommy glanced into his rear view mirror; he could see that Jill was busy doing something behind the truck.

"10-4 Gunny…Little Bear here…headed home to Jackson east bound 40, looking over my shoulder, all clear of super troopers all the way into Ole Miss…roger that? Over."

"10-4 LB, that's good news, appreciate the update. Gunner out."

Tommy got out and went to see what Jill was up to back behind the pickup "Whatcha doing baby girl?"

With a look of sarcasm on her face, Jill just looked at her father and went back to her work. It was now obvious as she was busy applying humorous bumper stickers that she bought at the Stop-N-Go to cover up the NRA and Patriotic stickers that lined the trucks rear bumper.

"Did you get a route?" she asked.

"I sure did, just like I thought. 40 to 240 around Memphis, then back on 40 west right into Little Rock, Arkansas, then pick up 30 west to Texarkana." Without saying another word, Jill just nodded and stepped back to admire her work. Where there was an NRA sticker was now one that read "Jesus is coming back…EVERYONE LOOK BUSY."

Looking at her father, Jill could see that he needed rest. "Dad you look exhausted. As long as the route is clear, why don't you let me drive for a while and you get some sleep?" Without saying a word Tommy handed the keys to Jill and walked to the passenger side of the truck.

Pulling out of the gas station, Jill turned the truck back to the 55 south entrance ramp; it was only about five miles before the I-40 interchange. Settling into the driver's seat, Jill merged into traffic behind a cattle truck that was doing about 70; she decided to keep her speed around 65 so as not to drawn attention to them. Turning to ask her father if he minded her turning the radio on, she heard a low snore and saw that he was already in a deep sleep. Jill lit a Marlboro and searched the radio unsuccessfully for something other than Christian or news to listen to, she decided on the propaganda news so she could update her father once he woke up.

"Once again we go to Craig Stephens for the latest…what have you got Craig?"

"Thank you Mathew, reports out of the pentagon say that an unarmed civilian aircraft has been shot down without warning over the breakaway rebel state of Texas killing all aboard!

No further details are available at this time. An unnamed but reliable source confirms that a private civilian jet, en route to Mexico, strayed into airspace that the rebels claim to be above their sovereign territory and was taken down by a SAM missile battery site located north of Fort Worth. Texas authorities claim that the flight was on a spying mission over sensitive military installations. Further statements say that any survivors will be put on trial for espionage; and if found guilty will be executed! Back to you Mathew."

"Thank You Craig. A statement from President Brown at the White House says he is deeply saddened by these tragic events and his prayers go out to the families and loved ones of those killed or injured, and that these acts of cowardice will not go unpunished. He also pleaded for calm, and for citizens not to engage in vigilante justice. We are also receiving reports from all over the country of mass protests against this violence, denouncing this as a way for Texas to escalate tensions between the government and the rebels. Reports are pouring in from New York, Boston, and Philadelphia, from Chicago and St. Louis, to Los Angeles and San Francisco."

Jill had heard enough. *She knew propaganda bullshit when she heard it.* Disgusted, she turned the radio off. *This was just another way for the government to spin the story to their advantage and advance their agenda.* Entering Mississippi, her thoughts again drifted back to her dream of the man she had served breakfast to seemingly years ago, but in reality it had only been a few days. *What was it about him? He seemed so sad that morning, yet she also sensed a quiet resolve, all business, like he had mission that he needed to complete.* But those were obvious observations with all that was going on that morning; *there was more to it than that, something intangible that made her take notice…but what? What possessed her to write her phone number on his receipt, what made her dream about him like she was a love-struck high school girl suffering from a crush? How would it feel to be held in his embrace, to passionately kiss, to make love to and…How sad, she thought, that she would never know the answers to these questions. Put it out of your mind, Jill thought, shaking her head to clear it of thought.* Looking over at her father still sleeping next to her, Jill decided to turn on the CB to listen to the chatter.

CHAPTER NINE

*The scientific man does not aim at an immediate result.
He does not expect that his advanced ideas will be readily taken up. His work is like that of the planter - for the future. His duty is to lay the foundation for those who are to come, and point the way.*

Nikola Tesla

DENNIS WAS SEARCHING FOR SOMETHING, BUT HE didn't know what. What was he looking for, where was he, where was he going? Scanning the faces of the people around him, nothing seemed familiar accept the smell of...

"Coffee?" Opening one eye, he could see Charley, pot in hand standing over him. "Coleman, you want some coffee?"

Nodding his head, Dennis let out a grunt, sat up and accepted the cup of steaming hot Joe that Charley poured and drained it in two gulps.

"More?" Charley asked, still standing over him.

Holding the cup out toward Charley, he said "Please." After refilling the cup, Charley placed it on the ground next to Dennis's bedroll He turned on his heel and returned to his place beside the campfire, where Jack was seated tending to the bacon frying in the pan.

Standing to stretch his legs, Dennis walked down to the stream to wash up and tend to other morning duties. Dipping his hands into the stream, he grabbed a handful and washed his face. The icy cold water immediately woke him up, it felt and tasted so fresh. Looking upstream, Dennis gazed toward the mountain tops in the distance. His thoughts were broken by a trout jumping and flapping at the water downstream. He would like to come back here and fish someday.

Following the aroma of maple cured bacon and coffee, he returned to camp. Dennis sat and began to eat. *So what was the plan for today?* He thought. Before he could ask, Charley, as if reading his mind, spoke.

"After you're done eatin', pack up your gear and go with Jack up trail and help him haul that second crate back here." *And what are you going to do?*

But again, before he could ask, Jack spoke. "That there is a rough trail, and he ain't in no shape to make it and haul that crate, so he'll stay back here and haul our gear back to the trucks and cover our sign." *Holy Shit...a whole sentence* he thought looking at Jack in amazement

"Any questions?" Charley asked.

Looking at Charley, he said "Yeah... how do shut him up?" pointing a thumb in Jack's direction. With that Jack stood up and with a wide grin crossing his face.

"OK Yank, let's getter goin'." With that, Jack walked into the brush with Dennis bringing up the rear. After a half an hour of cutting through thick briars, and climbing over countless dead-falls, Dennis noticed that Jack's pace had slowed considerably, stopping to look around and side to side, studying marks on tree trunks as if he were looking for something in particular.

Dennis didn't need to be told what his role was; his job was to be able to find their way back to camp, and since things look different on the way back he would use these opportunities to study the back trail. Coming into a narrow clearing, Jack stopped and pointed toward two small mounds about a quarter mile ahead and down the mountain side, it sort of looked like a...

"I'll be dammed." he said out loud, It looked like a camel's humps, just like Charley had said. "What now Jack?"

"Now we hike our way into the valley between the two humps and study for signs," he replied. After what seemed like an hour, they finally made their way into the valley.

"Look around" Jack instructed.

"What am I looking for?"

"Any unusual markings on tree trunks that looks old." With that, they went in separate directions. After about a half hour of searching, Dennis was becoming frustrated and sat down on dead fall to rest. Removing his cap he laid it next to him on the fallen tree and began to wipe the sweat from his forehead. Standing to resume his search Dennis bent down to retrieve his cap when he noticed what looked like a carved marking next to his cap.

Pointing down at the marks, Dennis called, "Jack! Over here."

Jack strolled over and studied the marks for about two seconds before slapping Dennis on the back. "Good job… how'd you find that?"

Laughing, Dennis replied, "I was literally sitting on it."

"You're kidding?"

Still laughing and shaking his head side to side, "No," was all he could say.

"Well that's using your brain Yank," Jack said with a laugh. Running his hand over the marks, he stepped back and surveyed the landscape. Scanning the area, his gaze stopped and he motioned for Dennis to follow him as he slowly walked toward a small outcrop of earth nestled dead center between a stand of three trees. "Let's dig." Four feet down they hit pay dirt; Jack had uncovered a box that looked very much like the one that Charley had been sitting on yesterday. Dennis lifted the box from the hole; it was fairly, but not overly heavy. He could see that it was quite old, but it was also very well built. Jack was already busy refilling the hole and doing his best to conceal any sign that anyone had been there. He walked back to the deadfall trunk, took out his knife, and began to alter the marks. Jack stood back to admire his work on the mound and tree trunk. Satisfied that he had covered their tracks, he sat down on the deadfall. "We'll rest a while before headin back."

Sitting next to Jack on the fallen tree, Dennis could no longer contain himself, but again before he could ask, as if he knew, Jack spoke first. "So ya wanna know what's in the box?"

Shaking his head in exasperation, he said "What is it with you two? That's really becoming annoying! Yeah I want to know."

Jack let out a loud laugh and said "You ain't the first sentinel we gone a'huntin with, ya know."

"So how'd I do?"

"Not bad for a yank, now go ahead and open the box."

With that, Dennis pried open the lid of the box to find about 100 bags, filled with what felt like coins. Opening one, he found each bag contained 50 one ounce gold coins. Each coin was marked "CSA," and dated 1863 with the image of Jefferson Davis on one side and the Confederate flag on the other. Doing some quick math in his head, he mumbled "That's 100 times 50 equals 5,000, at about $1,500.00 per ounce that's… HOLY SHIT!"

Dennis just looked at Jack who, as if on cue, said,

"Yup that's seven and a half million dollars."

Dennis again looked into the box and again at Jack as if he was waiting for the answer before asking the question. He stared at Jack and shrugged his shoulders as if to say… *Well?* Again Jack did not disappoint. "Before the war ended, the Rebs knew they couldn't win, so they set about hiding deposits of gold all over the south and west. They knew the day would eventually come when the government would again attempt to dictate power over the states, and subvert the Constitution and Bill of Rights. History teaches that the Civil War was fought over slavery. The truth is, it was fought over the individual states' rights to abolish slavery and determine that on their own without mandate by an overreaching federal government."

Almost not believing what he had just heard, Dennis could only stare at Jack in total amazement. *This whole dumbass country boy thing was all just an act!* As if sensing the light bulb going on in Dennis's head, smiling, Jack spoke again. "Now we can set here and jaw about southern history all day, but it's a getting' late and we still gots to hike a spell back yonder, an lotsa work to do!"

Reaching down to close the box, Jack grabbed a handle, looked up at Dennis and back at the other handle and again back at Dennis. Dennis reached down and grabbed the other handle. He could only grin as they began walking back up trail towards camp.

CHAPTER TEN

*My reading of history convinces me that most bad gov-
ernment results from too much government.*

Thomas Jefferson

President Brown picked up the receiver of the phone to
hear the familiar voice of his secretary. "Mr. President, Mr.
Epstein and General Crain are here."

"Send Meyer in." Meyer Epstein entered the Oval Office
to find the President studying the days' Intel reports.

"Good morning, sir."

"Morning Meyer, have you reviewed Crain's attack plans?
What do you think about these troop movements that he's
made?" "Well sir, it looks to me like he's found a weakness to
exploit, and is employing a diversionary action to draw support away from it."

"Well I've called him in to explain this before I approve it." Epstein poured himself a cup of coffee and sat in one of the chairs in front of the President's desk. Without making any eye contact, Epstein sat quietly sipping his coffee for a few minutes with a concerned look on his face. Brown finally broke the silence. "What's wrong Meyer?"

"Well sir … I'm not convinced that this is the wisest course of action," he replied.

"Why do you say that Meyer?"

Still looking down at the floor, Epstein took a moment, and continued to sip his coffee while trying to choose his words carefully before responding. Finally, looking the President dead in the eye, he spoke. "Mr. President."

Brown was always immediately worried when Epstein began with *Mr. President.*

"Let Texas go! Just let them and any others that want to join them go!"

Brown could not believe what he was hearing. He had never known Epstein to back down from a political fight before, he knew that he wasn't a coward; he was a pragmatist, and had never failed to give him sound political advice, but why at the most critical time now?

Brown just looked at him in stunned silence before uttering one word. "Continue."

"We should continue the path toward achieving our goals of world socialism through the slow process that we have successfully been employing, rather than armed conflict and open warfare that will only unite and harden the opposition. I firmly believe that this administration will go down in flames if we continue to follow this course. I think that you will go down in history as the man who ignited what has the potential to become a worldwide ideological conflict that ultimately causes the deaths of millions!"

Brown was without words. He knew Meyer was right, but he also knew that he had higher aspirations to become the leader of the new order; and that allowing such secession would be looked upon as a sign of weakness to harshly deal with any opposition. Slowly nodding his head, he finally spoke,

"Duly noted. As always, I appreciate your thoughts and advice and I will take it under consideration. Now, is there anything else?"

As if to say *what more do you want?* Exasperated, all Epstein could do was shrug his shoulders and say, "Not at this time Mr. President"

Again with the Mr. President…that's twice. Brown then reached over and activated the intercom.

"Yes Mr. President?"

"Send in General Crain."

Educate and inform the whole mass of the people...They are the only sure reliance for the preservation of our liberty.

Thomas Jefferson

With two crates of Confederate gold hidden beneath the false floor of his pickup, KGC sentinel Dennis Coleman made his way south on the back roads of Arkansas toward the Texas border, to a point on route 41 where he could slip into Texas to a town about 20 miles west of Texarkana called New Boston. There, he would make contact with other sentinels and be escorted to another undisclosed location to deliver his load.

New Boston. How ironic, he thought, that the first American Revolution began in Boston and a town named New Boston would become a major part of the second! His instructions from Charley were to monitor the CB radio and when he got close to the border, to a town called Foreman, make a call on channel 19 for driving information, using the CB handle "Goldilocks." He would then wait for an answer from "Guide Dog" for further instructions.

Driving at night, Dennis could not really view the scenery of the area but figured it would begin to look much like northeastern Texas. Searching the radio channels for any current news reports, he came across a reporter named Craig Stephens from NSMBA who was describing peaceful compliance of citizens turning in their firearms all across the country.

"Craig, Mathew Krys in New York here. We are getting reports of minor resistance and protests with relatively few people being taken into custody for opposing the President's Executive Order. Tell us, are you hearing the same thing?"

"Yes Mathew, some small protests have had to be put down and arrests have been made, but overall it has been embraced by the vast majority of the people!"

OH BULLSHIT, Dennis thought. He turned off the radio and switched on the CB.

"10-4 there Reaper 13, the latest is there have been mass protests in Tennessee, Kentuck, Bama, Ole Miss., Nebraska, New Mex., Arizona, Louisiana, Georgia, the Carolinas and all across the country! The National Guard is being used for crowd control, thousands of arrests have been made, which has led to violence between protesters and law enforcement and guard troops…word is that Alaska is preparing to also secede!"

"Roger that Crash Man. I heard pretty much the same, and the media is reporting nothing but a shit load of propaganda."

Two miles outside of Foreman, Dennis keyed the mic. "Break one nine for Goldilocks south bound on 40 lookin for a report." After a few seconds Coleman got the reply he was looking for.

A thick southern drawl boomed out of the speaker filling the cab of his pickup.

"Howdy there Goldie, this here is Guide Dog, what's your 20 come back?"

"Roger that Dog, on route 40 rolling into Foreman… over"

"Well if you're looking to fuel up and something to eat, there's a diner just south of Foreman that serves up good coffee and a damn fine biscuit and gravy breakfast. Ima headin that away myself."

Dennis lit a cigarette and replied. "Sounds like a plan to me, I am a bit hungry and I ain't had any good southern cooking for quite a while. Thanks for the tip, breakfast is on me."

"Roger that Goldie, that's a deal, I'll be seeing ya there."

Every citizen should be a soldier. This was the case with the Greeks and Romans, and must be that of every free state.

Thomas Jefferson

A small bump in the highway made Master Sergeant Tommy "Gun" Riley wake with a start. It was approaching dawn as Tommy surveyed the landscape, and the terrain was unfamiliar to him. Jill was concentrating on the road ahead and had not noticed that he was awake. She looked tired, but still showed the beauty that she had inherited from her mother; same eyes and nose, but with a slightly different hairline. He thought they probably could have passed for sisters.

Tommy shifted in his seat and felt the pain and heard the loud crack his stiff neck made from sleeping in a crooked position. *What the hell was he doing here;* he asked himself, *he should be enjoying life playing with grandchildren instead of driving a thousand miles to freedom…*this was not how he had envisioned spending his golden years! Without breaking her gaze from the road, Jill's voice broke the silence.

"Morning Dad, have a good sleep?" *Good sleep? Hell the last time he slept this bad was in Nam the day before his orders came through that his tour had ended.* Without answering her question, Tommy turned to look out the window to see a sign that read Prescott 3 miles.

"Where are we?"

"Just left Arkadelphia on I-30 south, about a hundred miles southwest of Little Rock and around 30 to 40 miles north of Texarkana."

Wow, he thought, I must have been out for a while. "You made good time, you want to stop and get some food and then I'll drive while you sleep?"

I could use a bit of both, she thought. "Sure. As soon as we cross into Texas we'll stop and get a bite."

Spotting the diner, Coleman could hear the tires growl as he pulled onto the gravel of the empty parking lot. So as to be able to see any approaching vehicles, Dennis backed into a spot alongside of the diner. After a few minutes, he decided to close his eyes to get a short cat nap; he awoke about ten minutes later to the sound of a passing rig, but still no Guide Dog. Now, listening to the silence of the morning, Dennis lit a smoke and leaned back in the seat to wait. A light fog was beginning to lift revealing the morning dew, and he could smell the aroma of the fresh biscuits that were baking inside the diner. Enjoying the smells, he took a long deep breath of the fresh clean air of rural south Arkansas. Much better than the smells where he lived, in a neighborhood nestled between an industrial area, a rail yard and an airport on the Southwest side of Chicago.

His thoughts wandered back a few days to where he had stopped for breakfast that morning, *Jill the waitress, the old man with the hat, the expressions on the customers' faces and the eerie quiet that filled the room with a deafening silence as they ate. Was it only four days ago? It seemed like much longer!* After about ten minutes he could see a truck approaching in the distance and watched as it slowed to turn into the gravel lot. Pulling up beside him, the driver leaned out the window.

"Morning, you Goldilocks?" Dennis just nodded his head. "Well I'm your Guide Dog, now let's get at those biscuits, you're buying!"

The cost of freedom is always high, but Americans have always paid it. And one path we shall never choose, and that is the path of surrender, or submission.

John F. Kennedy

Maneuvering his parachute, John "Eclipse" Michaels landed softly in an open field, in a valley surrounded by low hills on two sides. Once on the ground, as quickly as he could, Eclipse rolled up his chute and checked his compass. He would travel east to a predetermined extraction point at the Louisiana border. As he made his way toward the tree line at the eastern end of the valley, he could hear the unmistakable sound of the chopper blades of an approaching helicopter. Slipping into the trees he waited and scanned the sky until he spotted a Huey UH-1 coming in at low altitude from the northwest. Michaels waited until the chopper had passed his position before resuming his course toward Louisiana.

After walking about four miles, he came upon a small town; scanning the area he likened it to a typical Texas town…a combination gas station and diner, a small grocery store, and six or seven business buildings. Feed & Hardware, and a Town Hall/ Post Office with a sign that read "Gilmer." Pulling a map from his flight suit pocket, he figured he was approximately 12 to 15 miles northwest of the city of Longview. Eclipse decided to try and make his way south of Longview to I-20, and follow it east until he could cross into Louisiana west of Shreveport.

An hour after the Huey passed his position he again heard the sound of an approaching helicopter, this time coming from the south. He thought to himself *have I been spotted and the pilot alerted to make another sweep of the area?* Watching as the chopper made a low pass and circling near his position before resuming course to the north, Michaels decided to wait a while before continuing toward Longview. His thoughts returned to his encounter and conversation with "Ramrod," and what he must have been feeling as he was forced to shoot down a fellow pilot. *How would he feel if he was in that same situation?* Conflicted to say the least, but he would be compelled to do his duty and follow his orders. Sitting quietly beneath the trees, he thought he could hear the sound of muffled voices and footsteps in the brush not far away. Drawing his sidearm, Michaels attempted to slip back further into the trees and utilize whatever cover he could to avoid being observed. Silently waiting and listening, a loud voice came out of nowhere from behind him.

"Come on out now boy!"

Slowly turning his head, he saw three men with shotguns looking directly at him though the tree leaves. *SHIT,* he thought, *should I run, make a stand or surrender?* The first two options were out of the question so with his hands raised, Captain John "Eclipse" Michaels emerged from under the branches. Standing before him were three tall men who from the looks of them appeared to be farmers.

"I'm Captain John Michaels United States Air Force."

The tallest of the three men spoke first. "Yeah we know who ya are, hell you got half the people in Texas lookin fer ya…we bin alookin fur ya all day. I'm Sergeant Crowe of the Texas Militia."

"Well aren't you the lucky ones, how did you find me so fast?"

"Boy I bin smellin ya for an hour."

"Smelling me, how could you smell me… you don't look like an Indian."

"Well, I am part Cherokee." Turning his head and sniffing the air Crowe continued. "You smell like jet fuel, use Old Spice deodorant, you had maple flavored syrup on yer pancakes, and hickory smoked bacon with yer breakfast this morning. Hell son, I could find ya in the dark and I'm only one quarter Cherokee!"

Damn if he wasn't right.

Eclipse couldn't help but laugh and smile. "Ok so what now?"

"First hand me over that there sidearm and come with us."

"Where to?"

"Back up the road apiece to my truck and I'll radio the Longview police that we're abringin ya in, any more questions?"

Thinking for a moment Michaels replied, "Yeah, how's the coffee there?"

With a wide smile Crowe said, "Absolutely terrible."

CHAPTER ELEVEN

Let every nation know, whether it wishes us well or ill, that we shall pay any price, bear any burden, meet any hardship, support any friend, oppose any foe to assure the survival and the success of liberty.

John F. Kennedy

GENERAL JOE SCOTT RECOGNIZED THE CALLER ID ON his cell phone. "Hiya George, been a while, what's new with you? They keeping you busy at the Pentagon?"

"It *has* been a while huh Joe. Not much, just putting down the usual insurrection and rebellion, what have you been up to lately?" Crain sarcastically replied.

Laughing, Scott shot back with equal sarcasm, "Oh you know, same old grind; trying to stay busy preparing for an invasion from superior forces based on orders from a socialist dictator bent on our enslavement. So how are the wife and family?"

"Good. My daughter Mary is having another baby due in June, so the wife's all excited about that, buying clothes and toys and such," Crain said in a matter of fact tone.

"Well congratulations, please give her our best. So to what do I owe the honor of this call? Surely I assume not just to invite us to the baptism?"

"Of course you're invited, but first I thought we could play some Stratego."

"Sure. Why, have you grown bored of playing Battleship with Admiral Johnson? You might hurt his feelings, and you know how much he enjoys pushing his little ships around that big board," Scott again laughingly replied.

"Yeah well he'll just have to get over it because the current situation dictates an air and ground action!"

Continuing the game of cat and mouse, Scott responded "That sounds rather ominous, wouldn't you prefer a nice game of chess?"

Crain's tone now changed. "Actually I would, but under the existing conditions I think that is no longer possible!"

Joe Scott paused to gather his thoughts for a moment. "And where do you propose we should begin play?"

"Now that wouldn't be fair. And I know you just as well as you know me, and you know I always play fair. My function is to illuminate the terrain on which we find ourselves deployed! "Scott sat back in his chair and took a deep breath before asking one final question.

"When do you propose that we schedule this match?"

"Soon my friend, very soon!"

Battle is the most magnificent competition in which a human being can indulge. It brings out all that is best; it removes all that is base. All men are afraid in battle. The coward is the one who lets his fear overcome his sense of duty. Duty is the essence of manhood.

George S. Patton

Approaching the Arkansas/Texas border, Jill Riley could see what looked like a military road block up ahead. Nudging her father to wake up, she said "Dad, we got company."

Tommy Gun woke with a start. "What's going on?" As they got closer it was obvious that the National Guard was stopping vehicles and inspecting them before turning them around and not allowing them to enter Texas.

"What should I do?"

"Nothing, wait for them to tell you," he replied.

After about ten minutes of waiting their turn behind an 18-wheeler, a soldier approached the pickup. Bending over to speak to her, he knocked on the window. Jill could see the name tag over his shirt pocket. "Good morning Private Sullivan, what's going on?" Jill inquired with a smile.

The soldier spoke with a stern but even tone. "Good morning ma'am… may I see some ID, and please state your destination and business." he replied.

Digging into her purse to find her wallet, Jill handed over her driver's license as she spoke. "We're heading into Texarkana on our way to visit some family in Bedford."

"ID please sir." Opening his wallet, Tommy handed it to Jill, who then handed it to Sullivan. "Please remove it from the wallet ma'am."

Doing as she was instructed, Jill removed the driver's license from her father's worn and tattered wallet and turned it over to the soldier. Glancing at the ID's, he directed "Please proceed to the inspection area behind the building on the right."

Jill did as she was told, pulling into a lot behind a Quonset hut building and she and Tommy were escorted inside while the truck was inspected. Tommy sat on a chair with his head down while Jill watched through the window as two soldiers approached the pick-up to conduct their inspection. The two soldiers searched the cab, and finding nothing, proceeded to the

"ATTENTION!" Before them Jill could see that the sol-
had formed into two lines of ten men each, facing each
. Colonel Rogers spoke again loudly.

"PARADE   REST;   TROOPS   READY   FOR
ECTION SIR."

Looking at her father, Rogers asked, "Please do me this
r Sir." Tommy laid his hand on Rogers shoulder. "Of
e!" With that, Tommy "Gun" Riley led Colonel Rogers
one line and back up the other, pausing once to pat one
r on the chest and adjust his collar. Reaching the end of
w, Tommy turned on his heel.

The men snapped to as Rogers ordered "ATTENTION,
DY, AIM, FIRE!" With that, 7 soldiers fired into the sky.
DY, AIM, FIRE!" The soldiers again followed the com-
. A third command was given. "READY, AIM, FIRE!"
s then did a complete about face and said "For your fallen
des, SIR." He nodded his head as a lone bugler began to
aps. Awestruck, with tears in her eyes, Jill watched with
e she had never known before as her father turned to
he lowering of the American flag. Three soldiers care-
olded it and marched forward to present it to Colonel
s who then handed it to her father.

Sir, please accept this as a token from a grateful nation
r service!" Extending his arm and looking directly at Jill
ed, "May I escort you to your vehicle?"

rear to search the truck bed. Seeing an assortment of suitcases and boxes, they began looking though the suitcases. Finding nothing other than clothing and personal items, they then started searching the cardboard boxes, where they found more personal effects, some more clothing and some photo albums.

Jill was becoming angry by the way they were treating the belongings that she had skillfully packed for the trip south. At the bottom of the last carton, they came upon a small metal lockbox. Knowing exactly what they had found, Jill watched as both peered into its contents. At that point, one of the soldiers left and returned with what appeared to be an officer who removed the blue ribboned medal from its holder. Unknown to Jill, this revealed a folded piece of paper that was below it. The officer unfolded the paper and began to read.

RILEY, THOMAS, R. Rank and organization: Sergeant, U.S. Marine Corps, 3rd Battalion, 5th Marines, 1st Marine Division. Place and date: near the Demilitarized Zone, Republic of Vietnam, 30 July 1967.

Citation: For conspicuous gallantry and bravery at the risk of his life above and beyond the call of duty. While his company was conducting an operation along a narrow jungle trail, the leading company elements suffered heavy casualties when they suddenly came under extreme heavy machine gun and mortar fire from a well-concealed and numerically superior enemy force. Hearing the engaged marines' calls for reinforcements, Sgt. Riley quickly exchanged his rifle for a machine gun and several belts of ammu-nition, left the relative safety of his platoon, and unhesitatingly rushed forward to aid his comrades. Taken under intense enemy small arms fire at point blank range during his advance, he was wounded in both legs but returned fire, silencing the enemy posi-tion. As Sgt. Riley continued to forge forward to aid members of the leading platoon, he was again wounded from an exploding mortar shell and again came under heavy fire from two auto-matic weapons, which he promptly destroyed. Learning that there were additional wounded Marines further along the trail, he braved a withering hail of enemy mortar and small arms fire to continue onward. As he reached the position where the lead-ing marines had fallen, he was suddenly confronted with a bold frontal assault by 40 to 50 of the enemy. Totally disregarding his safety, he calmly established a position in the center of the trail and raked the advancing enemy with devastating machine gun fire. His ammunition now exhausted, his weapon now rendered ineffective, he picked up an enemy submachine gun and, together with a pistol seized from a fallen comrade, continued his lethal fire until the enemy was forced to withdraw. After hurling his last grenade at the retreating enemy, he radioed and directed a mor-tar barrage on the enemy's position and then rejoined his pla-toon. Sgt. Riley's daring initiative, bold fighting spirit, and selfless devotion to duty inflicted many enemy casualties, disrupted the enemy attack and saved the lives of many of his wounded comrades. His personal valor at grave risk to himself reflects

the highest credit upon himself, the Marine C
Naval Service.

The officer then seemed to give one
order, who then left while she watched the of
soldier begin repacking the boxes and suitca
Once completed, she watched the officer v
building. As he got closer, she could now m
was a Colonel. He stepped through the doo:
to the left. No longer concerned with what w
of the window, Jill's attention stayed on the o
talking on the radio. *What the hell was going*
herself. After a few minutes, the officer emei
and walked straight up to Jill and Tommy
front of her father. Looking up, Tommy "C
that the officer came to full attention and sa
to his feet, he returned the salute. Holding
Colonel Rogers then spoke.

"Sir, it is my pleasure to shake the ha
the Medal of Honor!"

With that, Tommy replied "Thank
shook his hand. Rogers then turned to Jill ;

"Ma'am, sir, please follow me." He le
doors of the Quonset hut. Once outside,
and a loud voice broke the silence.

Taking Rogers by one arm and her father with the other they slowly walked down the aisle between the soldiers who were now in full salute. Once they reached the truck, Master Sergeant "Tommy Gun" Riley executed a text book about face and returned the salute. Climbing into the passenger seat, Tommy heard Rogers give a finale command.

"OPEN THE GATE."

Again extending his hand, Tommy asked "Are we free to go?"

Smiling and shaking Tommy's hand, he said "Yes sir you are free to go. As far as I'm concerned you've earned the right to go anywhere you damn well please!"

Jill put the old pickup into gear and drove through the gate into the Republic of Texas.

The worst thing in this world, next to anarchy, is government.

Henry Ward Beecher

Surrounded by his cabinet, and his most trusted staff and advisors, President Brown sat at the center of the White House meeting room table. Turning to the Director of Homeland Security, Jeannette Lapatina, he inquired "Jean, bring us up to date."

She shuffled through the papers spread out before her. After a long pause she replied with a slight sigh, "Well sir, I'm afraid it's not good. The reports of the downing of our surveillance plane as an off-course civilian aircraft is being pushed hard by NSMBA and other media outlets that we have in the tank; however, polls show that the general civilian population aren't buying it and other media are beginning to question the authenticity of that report. The number of firearms that are being voluntarily surrendered is far below what our estimates had projected. We are getting reports that a significant number of the people are hiding and burying stockpiles of arms and ammunition, indicating noncompliance and possible outright revolt.

For a moment Brown, unblinking, just stared at her. "Go on."

Again looking at the file, she continued. "As we had hoped, the initial protests were small and controllable and the protest leaders were taken into custody and are currently being detained in secure locations to deter further demonstrations. Unfortunately it appears to be having the opposite effect. Incarcerating these leaders has led to a galvanizing of these groups, who are then combining with other groups and civilian militias. This has caused the protests to grow in size and number. We are beginning to see some dissention among our own party members in both the House and Senate, who are caucusing with the opposition. This is being reported on CSPAN in spite of our attempts to censor it; as a result of this censorship, the rest of the media is showing cracks in its support."

Saying nothing, Brown turned to Felicia Finch, his Attorney General. "Felicia, what is your assessment of the situation?"

"Mr. President it would seem that this will continue to snowball to a point that it will become uncontrollable. We can hold these people indefinitely without charging them, which will deny them due process as you laid out in your address to the nation. However, I believe that if we continue rigidly on this course, its' only effect will be to inflame the citizenry to increase resistance to such a degree that we estimate that we will have to arrest and quarantine approximately 60 percent of the population."

For a moment, Brown sat silent and stone-faced. Looking around the room for whom to query next, he caught the eye of Myer Epstein, whose expression gave away that "I told you so" look. Brown next turned to Secretary of Defense Nash Butler. "Nash?"

"We suspect that the weak area that we identified is a ruse by General Scott to draw us into a trap. We intend to feign an attack in order to draw the enemy focus away from our invasion landing forces on the gulf, at Corpus Christi, Texas City and Brownsville, just west of South Padre Island. Scott would then be forced to move his attention to an incursion of the 101st

Airborne Division paratrooper drop, coordinated with a landing force led by elements of the First Infantry Division, who will link up and take Houston and San Antonio, then drive north toward Dallas. Air power will only be employed by the use of F-16's as protection for our invading ground forces against any enemy air forces. No bombers will be used, as we do not intend to destroy American cities and risk heavy civilian casualties which would further enflame the situation."

A slight smile crossed Browns face before he asked, "So what's the bad news?"

A now grim-faced Nash replied, "Our men are anticipating some kind of action in response to Texas's secession, however, internal polling of our troops indicate that they do not look upon the opposing force as the enemy. Many are sympathetic to their cause. The thought of being ordered to fire upon fellow soldiers and U.S. citizens could be considered as an illegal and immoral order, and they may refuse to follow it. Morale is at an all-time low, so we cannot be certain what percentage of troops will flat out refuse, or desert and possibly join forces with the enemy."

"The United Nations already has troops strategically stationed across the country and is prepared to provide those forces to supplement any depletion of U.S. ground forces." interrupted U.N. Ambassador Patricia Bower.

Standing up and raising his voice for dramatic effect, "MR. PRESIDENT, THIS IS A DIRECT VIOLATION OF THE POSSE COMITATUS ACT AND WILL ONLY SERVE TO MAKE MATTERS WORSE! HOW FAR ARE YOU WILLING TO GO WITH THIS?" General Crain argued.

"The people be DAMNED! Forget the Constitution George, it will no longer apply or exist after martial law is declared, and we will go as far as we have to in order to lead us into the New World Order," Brown shot back.

Speaking for the first time, former Secretary of State Marjorie Holden Plimpton interjected, "I agree. At this point, what does it matter?"

All great change in America begins at the dinner table.

Ronald Reagan

"Howdy," came the greeting of the cook/waiter. The aroma of the fresh baked biscuits filled the air of the Foreman diner. A quick glance around the room revealed a typical old country diner with a counter, six tables and four booths, the walls decorated with the usual banners of the Dallas Cowboys and Arkansas Razor Backs, as well as photos of probably every high school football team since the town was settled. Two old time locals turned to see who had walked in. Seeing only a couple of strangers, the disappointment and disapproval was evident by their expressions, as they were probably expecting to see some other regulars to join their discussion.

So their conversation could not be overheard, they chose the booth farthest away from the kitchen area. Without so much as a word, Dennis and Guide Dog sat across from each other. As if on cue, the cook approached the table with a pot of coffee in his left hand, two cups and an ash tray in his right and a couple of menus tucked at his side. "Mornin' gents," he said, "biscuits will be done in five minutes." Setting the cups and ash tray on the table, he poured the coffee.

Amazed at the sight of the ash tray, Dennis asked, "I can smoke in here?"

Laughing at the question he replied. "Son, I'm Billy Joe, and this here is my place. We've been serving biscuits and gravy here for seventy years, and God willing, we'll be serving 'em for seventy more, and in all that time I say what ya can and can't do in my place. And nobody or no government gonna tell me different and that's the way it should be! You wanna smoke, go ahead and smoke, you wanna chew, I'll bring ya a paper cup to spit in, you wanna swear, go ahead and swear… just not too loud when kids or ladies are around. Act like a gent and you'll be treated like a gent. Thems my rules and if ya don't like 'em then take yer business elsewhere… there's another place about 40 miles down the road!"

A broad smile crossed Dennis's face as he reached into his shirt pocket, pulled out a smoke and lit it. Inhaling deeply he replied,

"Fair enough…two orders of biscuits and gravy with bacon."

If you can't feed a hundred people, then feed just one.

Mother Teresa

A strange voice broke the silence, "Wake up son, you hungry?" Eclipse opened his eyes and blinked. *Where am I?* He wondered. Thinking for a moment he remembered his encounter with Ramrod and ejecting, the relief he felt when his canopy opened, watching as his Raptor crashed into the field below, being captured, and the ride to Longview. Looking around he could see that he was in a typical tight lock-up cell with barred windows and doors, a couple of steel benches, a small table, sink and a toilet. Sitting up, and taking a moment, Eclipse tried to rub the sleep from his eyes and gather his thoughts. Speaking in a thick Texas drawl, again the voice asked,

"You hungry fly boy?"

Looking over his shoulder to see who was talking, Michaels saw a short, middle-aged, heavy-set man wearing a uniform, and a Deputy Sheriff's badge with a name tag that read "Johnson," holding a tray of food and smiling at him from the other side of the barred door.

Feeling the emptiness and growl coming from the pit of his stomach, Eclipse nodded his head. "I could eat." Standing to stretch out his legs and back, he quickly splashed some water from the metal sink on his face before approaching the bars.

"What time is it?"

Still smiling, Johnson replied "lunch time."

"So, Deputy Sheriff Johnson, what's on the menu today?" Michaels inquired in a matter of fact tone.

Pulling back the napkin revealing a plate of food that looked like it could be a photo from an issue of Country Kitchen magazine, Johnson said "Well son, you're getting the royal treatment. Miss Dee cooked you up a couple of chicken fried steaks with gravy, some corn and mashed tators, corn bread and coffee."

"Looks good!" Michaels exclaimed, as he accepted the tray through the slot in the door bars.

"Tastes better," came the reply.

Setting the tray on the small metal table, Michaels removed the napkin releasing the wonderful aromas that now filled the cell. Laughing to himself, he thought, *it wouldn't be difficult for Sergeant Crow to track these smells!* Sitting in silence, Eclipse sampled a bite from each item… Delicious! His face then contorted as he washed down a bite of corn bread with a sip of coffee. One thing was for certain, Crow was right about the coffee. Absolutely terrible!

CHAPTER TWELVE

In matters of style, swim with the current; in matters of principle, stand like a rock.

Thomas Jefferson

Sitting at his desk, President Jim Walter was busy reading the report of Captain Joe Glipski's shoot down of the F-22 Raptor that had violated Texas air space, including the search for, and eventual capture of the downed pilot, as well as his military dossier.

Captain John Michaels, born 7/8/82, entered military service 9/7/2000, after flight training, assigned to Nimitz super carrier CVN 76 USS Ronald Reagan 5/10/2003 thru 8/11/2007. Served two tours in Persian Gulf, currently assigned NAS Pensacola, Fla.

Reading the transcript of the radio conversation between Glipski and Michaels, it would seem that Captain Glipski gave him every opportunity to abort his mission, but was basically ordered by Michaels to follow the orders from his superiors. *Sounds like a good man,* Walter thought, *I'm glad he wasn't killed!*

Just then, the sound of Barbara Rae's voice over the intercom broke the silence in the executive office "Govern--" Catching herself, she corrected "Mr. President, Governor Katrina Gonzalez of New Mexico is on the line."

Walter picked up the receiver. "Good morning Governor Gonzalez, how are you today?"

"Fine, just fine Mr. President, and yourself? A bit busy I imagine!"

"What's with the Mr. President? You used to call me Jim."

Laughingly Gonzalez replied, "Well you used to call me Katy, but I believe that the circumstances have changed a bit don't you think?"

"I guess you could say that. Yeah, the situation has kept me a bit busy; I haven't had much time to do any fishing, but duty calls you know! So to what do I owe the pleasure of this call?"

"Well Jim, I just wanted to let you know that the people of New Mexico sympathize with your cause and support your actions. Also, I refused the military's request and attempt to place mobile armored and infantry units along our border with Texas. I have had conversations with Governors Kendal of Louisiana, Mesa of Arkansas, and Sherri Callon of Oklahoma, and we all agree that we will not support or allow any use of US, or any other multinational military forces to violate your borders from our respective states."

Walter paused for a moment.

"Well Katy, I appreciate that very much, you have no idea how glad I am to hear you say that," he replied with a sigh of relief.

Gonzalez continued. "I also speak for the other Governors when I say that the majority of our citizens are also in support, and we are all prepared, if necessary, to back Texas by whatever means, by use of our state guard and individual citizen militia groups, up to and including formally joining with you to preserve our state sovereignties."

As if a heavy weight had somehow been lifted from his shoulders, Walter paused and with an audible sigh responded, "It's very gratifying to hear that too Katy. For as Benjamin Franklin once said, we must all hang together or assuredly we shall all hang separately!"

The only thing that makes battle psychologically tolerable is the brotherhood among soldiers. You need each other to get by.

Sebastian Junger

The gate leading into Texarkana was guarded by a squad of Texas Rangers and militia. A tall, slender ranger stepped into the center of the road and held his hand up high; Jill Riley obeyed his command. "Halt!"

Walking toward the driver's window, with a tip of his hat he leaned in to speak. "Ma'am, sir, Colonel Rogers informed us of your arrival. Welcome to the Republic of Texas." Tommy and Jill both nodded.

"Thank you." she replied.

"I'm sorry for the inconvenience, but for our records, I just need to see some ID and know your destination, purpose, and expected length of your visit."

Handing over the identification, Jill replied. "Certainly: we are going to Bedford to stay with some relatives and we plan to stay permanently."

The Ranger quickly glanced at their Illinois driver's licenses.

"Long drive, huh, you must be tired."

"Yes we are, and we still have a few hours ahead of us. May we go now?"

Stepping back and motioning to raise the gate, he again tipped his hat as he said,

"Yes Ma'am, please drive safely!"

Ten soldiers wisely led will beat a hundred without a head.

Euripides

Coffee pot in hand, Billy Joe approached the booth where Dennis and Guide Dog had just finished eating. "More coffee gents?"

Draining the cup, Coleman held it up. "Please!"

Billy Joe filled both men's cups and asked, "How was everything, you like them biscuits there Yank?"

Reaching into his pocket, Dennis pulled a cigarette from his pack, lit it, looked Billy Joe straight in the eye and declared,

"Billy, those were some of the finest biscuits and gravy I ever had! How'd you know I was a Yank?"

Billy Joe just smiled a wide grin as if he was being told a joke that he already knew the punch line to, turned on his heel and walked back into his kitchen.

The emptiness in his stomach now satisfied, Dennis looked across the table to his guide. "So what's next?"

"After we leave here you follow me on the back and farm roads and cross the Texas border. From there we part company and you go through New Boston to I-30 West toward Dallas. From there, you make your way to ATT Stadium, you know, where the Cowboys play. Tell the guard you have a package for Jeff Davis to deliver and he'll direct you where to go."

Understanding his instructions, Dennis had to laugh as he nodded his head,

"Jefferson Davis… so much for cloak and dagger huh?"

Guide Dog only shrugged his shoulders and said,

"Well, once we get you into Texas it's all good, right?"

"Yeah, I guess so," Dennis replied. With that they both drained their cups and got up to leave. Catching Billy Joe's eye, Dennis waved a twenty and laid it on the table.

Coming out of his kitchen Billy Joe stopped them at the door.

"Y'all come back now," he said with a wink of his eye, extending his right hand to Dennis and pointing his thumb to Guide Dog. "Any friend of his is a friend of ours!"

Taking his hand in a firm grip, Dennis replied, "I'll be back, you can bet on it!"

Stepping out the door, he looked around; the fog had lifted completely and only the dew remained. Stubbing out the cigarette butt with the toe of his boot, Dennis and his guide walked across the gravel lot toward his pickup. Next stop, Texas!

It was my duty to shoot the enemy, and I don't regret it. My regrets are for the people I couldn't save: Marines, soldiers, buddies. I'm not naive, and I don't romanticize war. The worst moments of my life have come as a SEAL. But I can stand before God with a clear conscience about doing my job.

Chris Kyle

Asleep in his Longview cell, the silence was broken by the voice of Deputy Sheriff Johnson. "Wake up fly boy, your ride's here, time to go son."

Captain John Michaels awoke to the unmistakable sound of the whirl of helicopter blades cutting through the air approaching from the distance. Rubbing his eyes, he stood and stretched his limbs that were stiff from sleeping on the steel bench. Searching his thoughts, Eclipse asked, "Where am I going now?"

"Beats the hell outta me, I just work here, I was told to get you ready for transport," Johnson replied. "Just put on a fresh pot… y'all want some coffee before you go?"

Laughing to himself, Michaels could only respond with an emphatic "NO!"

With that, Deputy Johnson pushed his key into the lock, and with the stereotypical squeak you hear only in movies, opened the cell door. Escorted by Johnson and another deputy out to the parking lot, they marched toward the waiting chopper. Before boarding, Michaels turned, offered his hand to Johnson and said, "You be sure and thank Miss Dee for that fine meal."

Once he was seated and belted in, the rotors began to pick up speed for lift off. Eclipse yelled to Johnson, "HEY DEPUTY, ONE SUGGESTION… FROM NOW ON LET SOMEONE ELSE MAKE THE COFFEE!"

The BBC cameraman held up his hand and counted down… 3, 2, 1, then pointed his finger. "This is Nigel Collin reporting from Rosewood, a small town just north of Big Sandy; the site of the downed U.S Air Force F-22 Raptor in the breakaway American state of the Republic of Texas. Initial reports from the American press that an off-course commercial plane had been shot down have proved to be false." As the camera panned across the wreckage, Collin continued.

"With us now is Texas Guard pilot Captain Joe Glipski, who has been credited with shooting down the intruding aircraft. Captain Glipski, do you have any regrets about having to fire on a former brother U.S. pilot?" Collin tilted his microphone toward Joe as the cameraman zoomed in for a close-up of Ramrod.

"Sure I had some conflicts, I had hoped he would have let us escort him out of our airspace, but I also had my orders, as did he. But I was also very relieved when I saw him eject and the canopy of his chute open."

Collin continued his questioning. "Were you aware that he had been captured unharmed?"

A look of relief crossed Ramrod's face. "No I was not, but I'm very happy to know that."

"Also with us is one of the men responsible for capturing the downed pilot, Sergeant Crowe of the Texas Guard Militia. Sergeant, how were you able to find this pilot so quickly?"

With more than a hint of sarcasm a smiling Crowe replied. "Well they ain't many people walkin' around in East Texas wearin' a flight suit, so that kinda narrowed it down a bit."

"Did he resist capture in any way?"

"Nope… he seemed like a pretty nice fella for a Yankee boy."

Not knowing what else to say to make this interview more interesting, Collin was saved by the sound of the approaching helicopter. The BBC camera panned to the right just in time to record the chopper touching down about 35 feet away. Raising his voice to overcome the volume of the spinning rotor and pressing his earpiece tighter for dramatic effect, he continued.

"I'm being told that the pilot is being airlifted to the crash site. Hopefully we will be able to have a few words with him."

Within a few seconds, the chopper door opened and John Michaels stepped out into the Texas field. He was immediately escorted to the wreckage of his F-22 where, under the watchful eye of an officer of the Texas Air Guard, he was allowed to scrounge through the debris of what was left of the cockpit. Eclipse soon found the photo of his wife and son he was looking for and quickly stuffed it into the pocket of his flight suit. As a final farewell, Michaels gave the fuselage one final pat before being led to the waiting news crew. Eclipse immediately recognized Crowe, smiled and shook his hand. Leaning in toward Michaels, Crowe sniffed.

"Miss Dee's chicken fried steak huh?" To which Eclipse could only nod and smile.

Looking directly into the camera, Collins began his interview. "With us now is the pilot of the United States Air Force jet, Captain John Michaels." Turning to face Eclipse, he continued.

"Captain Michaels, how have you been treated since your capture?" Collin leaned the microphone toward Michaels.

"With a good meal and some awful coffee," he replied. Unable to contain himself, Crowe broke out into laughter. Not waiting for formal introductions, Michaels turned to Glipski, saluted and extended his hand.

"You must be Ramrod, nice to meet you Joe."

Returning the salute, Ramrod took Eclipse's hand in a firm grip as he replied "I am. You have no idea how glad I am that you're ok."

Eclipse responded with a smile. "Well, only because of your marksmanship. Taking out my right wing engine was some good shooting!"

Ramrod laughingly replied, "Not really... I was aiming for the left."

A politician needs the ability to foretell what is going to happen tomorrow, next week, next month, and next year. And to have the ability afterwards to explain why it didn't happen.

Winston Churchill

In stunned silence, President Brown sat back into the sofa as he watched the BBC report from Texas in the White House residence. Surrounded by his wife Estelle, Chief of Staff Meyer Epstein, and personal advisor Mallory Garrett, Brown looked to Epstein for advice. "Well?"

Taking his cue, Epstein offered his opinion. "Well it shakes out like this. Your administration has just been caught in an outright lie and exposed by one of the world's most highly respected news sources. If you are to continue on this course we need to spin this in a way that the public will accept, but how?"

"We can always say that it was a matter of national security" Garrett opined.

To which Epstein quickly retorted, "That would be seen as nothing more than propaganda! We need to change the narrative to galvanize public sympathy. As if we didn't want to release the truth until we knew what the pilot's status and condition were before notifying his family, followed by a tearful, heartfelt sympathy call to his wife inviting her to the White House, thanking him for his heroic service and her sacrifice, blah, blah, blah, and possibly a photo op with her and their kids."

"Do they have kids?" Brown asked.

"Yeah a 4 year old boy, that's something the public could relate to, and the press would eat it up!"

Estelle excitedly injected, "Ooh I like that…you could present a medal to the son as he salutes you, like John John Kennedy saluting JFK's casket during the funeral parade, there wouldn't be a dry eye in the country!"

Brown just gave her a stupid look and said, "but the man's not dead!"

To which she replied, "Who fucking cares? That's just semantics."

Meyer Epstein could only shake his head in disbelief as if he could not believe what he was hearing.

Every man has his own destiny: the only imperative is to follow it, to accept it, no matter where it leads him.

Henry Miller

Dennis Coleman entered Texas west of New Boston by way of a small farm road that crossed the border from Arkansas. His apprehensions having lessened now that he had entered Texas, he thought he might enjoy some casual conversation. Dennis keyed his CB mic. "Anybody got a traffic report for Goldilocks? Southbound on 30 from Texarkana to Dallas, come back."

"Roger that Goldie, heading that way myself toward Big D, 10 miles southwest of Texarkana… Looks good so far, last report we had was smooth sailing all the way. What's your 20? OVER."

"Just passed mile marker 195," Dennis replied.

"Looks like we're a few miles ahead of ya son," the man replied.

"You don't sound like a Texan, where ya'll from? OVER." Dennis queried.

"Born and raised in Hoosierville, then moved to the Land of Lincoln when I got out of the service," came the reply. "How about you son, what brings you here?"

Still being a bit guarded, Dennis paused for a moment before responding.

"Making a delivery in Dallas, I'm not sure what I'm gonna do after that. I might like it here and choose to stay, don't know what God has in store for me so I guess I'll just have to wait and see what happens."

"Well if I've learned one thing in my time, it's that if you're letting the Lord guide you, you can't go wrong!"

Dennis considered that for a few minutes before the man came back with "Did I lose ya Goldie, are you still there? OVER."

"Yeah I'm still here…Was just thinking about what you said there partner. I suppose you're right; I guess I just have to have faith that he'll put me where I need to be when I need to be there."

"Roger that Goldie sounds like a plan to me. It was good enough to get me outta some scrapes and back home and during the war, OVER."

"Are you a Nam vet?" Dennis asked.

After a short pause he replied in an exasperated tone, "Yeah, did a couple of tours… God-awful place, nothing but jungle, bad food and worse weather!"

Coleman continued the conversation. "What branch?… Were you in combat?"

"Marine Corps, Yeah saw some action…saw enough to know I never wanted to see any more," came the reply.

"How about you son, were you in the service?"

Again Dennis keyed his mic. "Semper Fi, huh, yeah, I did four years in the Army as a motor pool and tank mechanic in 1st Infantry Division."

"Big Red One, lots of history there son!" He responded in admiration.

Immediately Dennis's thoughts went back to his days during basic training when the sergeants constantly drilled that history into them on a daily basis.

"Yeah, the noncoms made us aware of that quiet often!" he replied with a laugh.

"I'm sure they did, that's their job! Well son, we're gonna pull in at this food and fuel stop for awhile, you're more than welcome to join us. COME BACK."

That's not a bad idea, Dennis thought. "I would love to continue this because I sure did enjoy the conversation and I appreciate the offer, but I really need to finish my business and make this delivery, so I'm gonna have to pass, but you take care now and drive safe OK! Goldilocks OUT."

"Right back atcha Goldie, God speed! Tommy 'Gun' Riley, OVER AND OUT."

Conservative, n: A statesman who is enamored of existing evils, as distinguished from the Liberal who wishes to replace them with others.

Ambrose Bierce

"The House will come to order!" Speaker Rainer bellowed as his gavel hit its mark with three loud bangs.

On the right side of the aisle a lone man rose to his feet and yelled, "Mr. Speaker!"

Finding the source of the voice Rainer answered, "The Chair recognizes the gentleman from Arizona."

"Mr. Speaker, I stand before you and this body today to voice my grave concerns for the future of our nation! With the signing of his executive order, the President, with the stroke of a pen and his cell phone, has basically torn up our Constitution and Bill of Rights. He has rendered Congress and the Supreme Court ineffective, and has consolidated all power to his control."

Interrupted by applause, after a short pause the gentleman continued. "Mr. Speaker, I have been inundated with calls and emails from a multitude of my constituents who have had friends and family members taken into custody, had their homes searched without warrants, their property confiscated, and have been denied due process according to law!" Once more applause interrupted the gentleman.

Now raising his voice to be heard above the cheers, he again addressed the chair and pointed his finger at Rainer. Waving his hand across the room, he said

"Mr. Speaker, my fellow colleagues, I have conferred with some of you from both sides of this aisle who have had similar complaints from the citizens in your states and ask that you now rise in a show of solidarity to this administration!" He shouted and pounded his desk on each point for effect, "THAT THIS BODY, AND THE AMERICAN PEOPLE, SHALL NOT STAND BY AND IDLY WATCH, AS OUR VALUES AND VERY WAY OF LIFE ARE THROWN ASUNDER ONLY TO BE REPLACED BY A TOTALITARIAN DICTATORSHIP!"

At that point all the members of the right wing as well as many on the left, along with the entire gallery rose and wildly cheered and applauded the statesman from Arizona. For several minutes, Rainer just looked around the room, refusing to call for order, allowing it to quiet down on its own. Choosing now to lower his tone, the gentleman continued.

"Mr. Speaker, in the words of Thomas Jefferson, 'when the people fear the government, there is tyranny. When the government fears the people, there is liberty.' In reading the Federalist Papers, we see that over two hundred and forty years ago when writing the Declaration of Independence and our Constitution, our founding fathers debated these same points. They rightly predicted that we again would come to this moment in history and endeavored to provide safeguards to prevent such tyranny from taking root!"

Pausing to let that thought sink in, the gentleman again continued his oratory.

"And so to my esteemed colleagues, ladies and gentlemen, and visiting members of the gallery I now say unto you," his voice now rising as he hammered away, again invoking the words of Thomas Jefferson. "A Bill of Rights is what the people are entitled to against every government and what no just government should refuse or rest on inference!" Pausing to look around the room, he continued.

"We now stand on the threshold of history, we stand at the precipice of an open and armed revolt not seen in this country for over one hundred and fifty years, and so I ask you, my colleagues, to stand up, to stand with me, to stand with your constituents, to stand up for the principals that make up the foundation of our democracy. Let us not tear open the scars nor reopen the wounds of our great national tragedy that was the Civil War, which pitted father against son and brother against brother; but let us come together as Dr. Martin Luther King envisioned when he said 'I have a dream that my four little children will one day live in a nation where they will not be judged by the color of their skin, but by the content of their character.'

Let us not be defined as a nation so divided by the political forces that conspire to keep us separated, but united by our common hopes and dreams for the futures of our families and our children!

Let us have the vision to recognize these forces for what they are, malignant growths on the body politic, and cut them out before they can invade and destroy all that surrounds it! Let us now heed the words of John Fitzgerald Kennedy who inspired us with these words."

"Let us not seek the Republican answer or the Democratic answer, but the right answer. Let us not seek to fix the blame for the past. Let us accept our own responsibility for the future."

His voice now rising to a crescendo, he thundered away as he pointed, "I NOW ASK YOU, AND YOU, AND YOU! WILL YOU RISE UP TO THIS CHALLENGE? WILL YOU PICK UP THIS STANDARD AND SCREAM IN ONE VOICE UNITED THAT TYRANNY SHALL NOT REIGN IN THE LAND OF THE FREE?"

Pausing to take a deep breath he screamed to be heard above the cheers, as he concluded, "THE EYES OF OUR FOREFATHERS ARE UPON US! THE EYES OF THE WORLD ARE UPON US! AND THE EYES OF HISTORY ARE UPON US TO REJECT THE EVIL FORCES OF SOCIALISM AND OF COMMUNISM THAT SEEK TO DIVIDE US, TO RISE AS ONE NATION AND DECLARE AS ONE PEOPLE THAT IN THE MELTING POT THAT IS AMERICA THAT BLACK LIVES MATTER, THAT WHITE LIVES MATTER, THAT

LATINO LIVES MATTER, THAT RED, YELLOW AND BLUE LIVES, MATTER. THAT CHRISTIAN, MUSLIM AND JEW LIVES MATTER, THAT STRAIGHT, GAY AND LESBIAN LIVES MATTER, BUT ABOVE ALL ELSE AMERICAN LIVES MATTER!"

CHAPTER THIRTEEN

*We have war when at least one of the parties to a conflict
wants something more than it wants peace.*

Jeane Kirkpatrick

WATCHING THE C-SPAN COVERAGE OF THE DEBATES
on the floor of the House of Representatives from the Oval
Office, Brown looked to Epstein for advice. "What do you
think Meyer?"

Epstein took his time to gather his thoughts before
answering. After a few moments of weighing out all the options
and possible scenarios, he finally spoke.

"Well sir the way I see it, you still have only two available options. First, is damn the torpedoes, full speed ahead and
continue on this course and all it entails; which in my opinion
would amount to political suicide, and would further escalate

civil rebellion and continued erosion of support from the party and media."

Pondering this for a moment, Brown swiveled in his chair to look out the window "Or?"

"Or second, you call for an emergency joint session of Congress and the Supreme Court and broadcast live on all the networks and attempt to de-escalate the situation with a mea culpa. Offer to rescind your executive order, thus restoring the Constitution and Bill of Rights, provided that Congress takes steps to enact strict gun control measures which we draft, that would restrict private firearm ownership to only those that meet stringent requirements. You would then invite Governor Walter to a summit and ask him to avoid taking any steps that cannot be recalled in an effort to resolve our differences so that Texas may peacefully regain its place among the states and rejoin the union. This will make you look presidential; in that you are showing a willingness to admit your decision was based on emotions tied to the latest tragedy and that you are reaching out to the opposition to compromise. This will show your humanity, which will shore up support from your base as well as the moderates and the media and help you regain your political footing."

Brown pondered his options. As it was not in his nature to be pragmatic he did not like the second, but he respected

Meyer's advice and needed to give it careful consideration. Brown decided to play devil's advocate. "What if Texas refuses?"

Without hesitating Epstein replied, "Again you have two options. You still have option one, but now it would be seen as a last resort measure to preserve the union, or two, just let them go!"

Brown immediately shot back, "wouldn't that embolden sympathetic states to follow suit?"

To which Epstein replied, "In that case, we enact a series of tariffs and trade restrictions that make it as difficult as possible for them to conduct commerce and do business. Hopefully this would discourage other states from seceding."

Again Brown carefully considered Meyer's assessment. Reaching for the intercom, his secretary answered "Yes Mr. President."

"Get General Crain!"

America lives in the heart of every man everywhere who wishes to find a region where he will be free to work out his destiny as he chooses.

Woodrow Wilson

Jill and Tommy walked into the fuel stop diner and were ushered to a table opposite the entrance. Taking their seats, Jill noticed that from this position she had full view of the customers who had taken up temporary residence in the restaurant. Seemed like the typical crowd of truckers, travelers and locals that are common to fuel stop diners that she had served back in Illinois. Her thoughts then reverted to the tall man that she gave her phone number to. *I wonder what he is doing right now, is he working? Why hadn't he called, did he lose the stub she wrote the number on? Was he married, or just not interested?* She pondered the question a few moments before her concentration was broken by the thick Texas accent of the waitress.

"Afternoon folks, I'm Linda and I'll be your server today," she said, as she offered them menus and filled their coffee cups without even asking. Looking up, Jill's gaze fell directly onto Linda's face; she quickly sized her up, mid-twenties, slim, shoulder length brownish blonde hair with a genuine smile.

Taking the menus, Jill returned the smile and inquired, "Hi Linda, what do you recommend?"

"Well the specials are on the inside, but our BBQ pork sandwich with baked beans and coleslaw is very good…ya'll need a few minutes?"

"That sounds good to me." Noticing that her father had not said a word but seemed deep in thought, Jill asked, "Dad, cheese burger with fries?" Tommy just nodded his head in approval.

Linda wrote it on her order pad, and said "coming right up." Then as quick as a cat, she turned on her heel in a way only another waitress could appreciate and moved on to the next table to refill their cups before disappearing through the kitchen doors.

Jill sipped her coffee and studied her father's furrowed brow. Snapping her fingers to get his attention… "Earth to DAD… Something wrong?"

Turning his head to Jill he replied,

"I was just thinking about the conversation I had with that guy on the CB."

Jill had been concentrating on driving and wasn't paying any particular attention to their conversation

"What about it?"

Thinking for a minute, Tommy replied,

"He said he would just have to have faith that the Lord will put him where he needs to be when he needs to be there!" Still staring off into space, Tommy paused and took a deep breath before he continued.

"I guess I never thought of it like that but I suppose that is why he put me on that trail in Nam at that place and at that time. I always figured it was my training and instincts that took over during that fire fight, to call me to do my duty."

Amazed and not wanting to interrupt, Jill could only sit silently listening. She had never heard her father utter a single word about his war experiences before now.

"Those were my boys out there, and I couldn't just leave them there to die!"

Jill could the see the look of sadness on her father's face and tears forming in his eyes. Turning to look his daughter straight in the face, and in a tone that trailed off into nowhere he said,

"I just pray that there is a purpose for us here and now, that he is guiding us to be where we need to be, when we need to be there. Looking away, his voice now lowered to an almost inaudible whisper. "Honey, war is a terrible thing!"

The object of war is not to die for your country but to make the other bastard die for his.

George S. Patton

Sitting quietly at his desk, General George Crain pondered what lay ahead, considering every different scenario and what they would mean to the future of the country. On the one hand, he could follow the orders of whatever course of action the President decided to employ, regardless of his agreement or disagreement. Or on the other hand, reject and refuse to carry out those orders if they conflicted with his principles.

As a career military man, he understood that his job was to follow policy, not make it. But it was also his job to advise and influence that which goes into making those policies that would enable him to enforce them. *How many hundreds of times as cadets had he and Scott, after playing Stratego or chess, taken turns playing devil's advocate while referring to each other as opposing generals, with Scott being Robert E. Lee, and Crain being Ulysses S. Grant, during debates of Civil War battles of these very questions at West Point? Why did you do this or that? What were you thinking when I did this?* Once Crain would take a position, Scott could be counted on to offer a wrinkle, or a "what if" to the equation that could alter the position and possibly change the outcome. Sometimes, halfway through the game, they would turn the board around and continue to play the other man's strategy. *What would he do if this situation were reversed?* The silence was broken by the voice of his secretary.

"General, the President is on the line."

Crain lifted the handset from its cradle, "Yes Mr. President."

Brown answered in an unfamiliar tone.

"General, I have made a decision. It is my decision and I take full responsibility for it. You are to implement your invasion plans per our discussion!"

"Yes Mr. President, although I must remind you that this decision legally constitutes a declaration of war, and this kind of order must be submitted in writing above your signature."

"Don't worry George, you'll have your written orders when I announce to the people and Congress. Keep me advised."

"Yes Sir, goodbye."

Crain sat back in his chair, and reminisced how he and Scott would speak to each other in a code that only the other understood. He had a decision to make and wished he could talk to his friend now. He might need to use that code again.

The end of labor is to gain leisure.

Aristotle

Driving west-bound on I-30, also known as Tom Landry freeway, Dennis spotted the sign he was looking for. *ATT stadium exit Texas 360 south.* His MapQuest directed him to then travel west to Randol Mill Road. Upon his arrival, the instructions from Guide Dog were to pull into the parking area, and then to security where he would be told where to make his delivery. Finally, he was approaching the end of his journey. "What will I do after this?" he wondered out loud.

Spotting the security sign pointing straight ahead, Dennis stopped at the gate shack; a short, overweight man in a guard uniform stepped out and approached his window.

From the appearance of his facial skin, which could only be described as wrinkled leather, he looked to be somewhere in his late seventies. Taking a rag from his pocket, he removed his Dallas Cowboys cap, revealing his balding head that was already producing beads of perspiration. He wiped his head and face and announced,

"How do? Hot one today huh!"

The name tag over his left shirt pocket said Homer, and Dennis's first thought was *"I hope that's his last name and not his first."*

"What can I help ya with son?"

"Special delivery for Jeff Davis" he replied.

"Another one? That man's sure been busy, you boys been showin up here from all over the country with special deliveries for him. This makes about a dozen so far this week!"

Dennis just shrugged his shoulders and said "Just doing my job."

"I reckon so," Homer replied, "I'll phone them and let them know you're coming. Just follow the signs that say *deliveries to the dock* and ask for Jeff." With that, Homer stepped back into the shack and opened the gate.

Dennis drove straight ahead and followed the signs around the back until he saw the deserted dock area. As he approached, one of the dock doors began to open revealing the figure of a man waving him in and pointing to the right. Dennis did as he was instructed, and entered the cavernous interior of ATT Stadium. After entering, he could see a man driving a fork lift toward him and gesturing for him to stop.

"I'm Jeff Davis, and you must be Goldilocks."

"How did you know that?"

With an expression that said *how do you think?* a smiling Davis just looked at him. "Coleman, right? Been expecting ya, you're the last one here."

"Hope I didn't keep you waiting."

"Nah" Davis replied, "You had the farthest to travel. Now, let's get you unloaded."

Followed by Davis on the fork lift, Dennis walked to the rear of his pickup, opened the tail gate and the panel that revealed the false bottom compartment that contained the two crates of confederate gold, and loaded them onto the fork lift. Davis then scribbled something onto a piece of paper on a clipboard and handed it to Dennis. "Sign this."

Taking the clipboard, he read the delivery receipt and signed, Dennis "Goldilocks" Coleman. Handing it back, Davis then tore off the top copy and gave it to Dennis.

"What now?" he asked.

Pointing toward an office doorway, he said, "Take that delivery ticket and all your fuel, and food receipts to that office, they'll issue you a pay check, and reimburse you for your expenses."

"And then what, will I get another mission?" Dennis questioned.

"Well that depends on you. Are you staying here, or going back home? If you're heading back, the bank will cash the check into U.S dollars. If you're staying, they will issue you cash and convert all your U.S. currency into Texas Bank notes. We've made arrangements for all you sentinel boys to stay at a nearby Holiday Inn where you can get cleaned up, sleep in a bed, get a good hot meal and relax by the pool for a few days."

That sure sounded good, but Dennis had to ponder the question for a minute before replying. "I haven't completely made up my mind yet."

Davis just nodded in understanding and said, "Well if you want my advice, you'll go to the hotel and think it over for a few days, I'm sure you'll make the right decision."

CHAPTER FOURTEEN

For in reason, all government without the consent of the governed is the very definition of slavery.

Jonathan Swift

"This is Mathew Kris, live from NSMBA studios in New York, where we are awaiting President Brown to address the nation before a joint session of Congress on a matter of national urgency. As of this minute, we have not been advised on what this will address, however, there is speculation that it will concern the growing number of protests, arrests and seizures that have taken place since the President signed his executive order banning the private possession of firearms.

Reports are coming in from all over the country of citizens hiding arms and ammunition and joining up with local citizen paramilitary militia units, and skirmishes with law enforcement and National Guard units. We now go to Craig Stephens, who is reporting from the border between New Mexico and Texas. Craig what do you have for us?"

"Well Mathew, this is a live shot of the dozens of vehicles full of people that are exiting Texas as opposed to the hundreds of cars and trucks that are lined up and being denied entry into that breakaway state. In an ironic turn of events, we are also getting reports from the border areas between Mexico and Texas that Mexican citizens that are seeking to reenter Mexico from Texas, and are being turned away by Mexican authorities that have constructed a fifteen foot fence topped with barbed wire as a barrier to prevent any illegal reentry."

"Craig this is Mathew; from what we are seeing this looks very similar to the exodus of refugees attempting to escape civil wars in Syria and the Middle East into Europe."

"Yes Matthew that is exactly what it feels like. Our attempts to interview the Texas Guardsmen that are manning these checkpoints have been denied, and they would only reply with 'no comment.' The bigger concern right now is the growing tension caused by the intrusion of a U.S aircraft into Texas air space that was shot down. The large numbers of news helicopters in the area, are being warned off by patrolling Texas Air Guard helicopters. They are also warning the U.S military aircraft in proximity not to approach or cross into Texas air space, and there is the possibility of an accident that could quickly escalate into armed conflict!"

"The good news is that we have received confirmed reports from multiple reliable sources from the International Red Cross that the downed U.S pilot has been confirmed as U.S. Air Force Captain John Michaels. At this time, he has been released to International Red Cross representatives."

Kris interrupted, "We now break away from Craig's report to the House of Representatives where President Omar Brown is about to enter."

We are fast approaching the stage of the ultimate inversion: the stage where the government is free to do anything it pleases, while the citizens may act only by permission; which is the stage of the darkest periods of human history, the stage of rule by brute force.

Ayn Rand

The Sergeant-at-Arms stepped through the open doors of the House chamber and bellowed, "Ladies and Gentlemen, the President of the United States." The usual obligatory applause was cut short; as a shocked Congress watched the President follow openly heavily armed Secret Service agents into the chamber. Brown appeared to be stern and deadly serious as he did not pause to exchange greetings or shake any hands, but quickly walked down the aisle to take his position below and in front of the Vice President and Speaker of the House. Reading from a written prepared speech, and not using a teleprompter, he began.

"My fellow citizens," he said. "I now come before this body to announce that by the powers granted to me as Commander In Chief in times of national emergency, as of today I am imposing martial law and have given orders to General George Crain to command our military to employ whatever resources, and by whatever means necessary to put down the insurrections across our nation, as well as to put down the rebellion of the state of Texas to secede from the union. These actions will include the use of United Nations forces in conjunction with National Guard and U.S military units, as well as local law enforcement, to enforce a strict dusk until dawn curfew for anyone that cannot show cause, such as work related or medical emergencies, and must produce proper identification or face indefinite detainment."

Brown continued. "Furthermore, Congress and the judicial branches, including the Supreme Court, are hereby and immediately suspended indefinitely. The executive branch shall retain complete and full authority to direct all federal agencies as well as all state and local government authorities, who will report directly to FEMA and the NSA for instructions and a full media blackout will be observed."

For a brief moment, a stunned Congress sat quietly until a lone yell of "TRAITOR" broke the deafening silence! A chant of "TREASON, TREASON, TREASON" erupted from both sides of the aisle. Stepping down from the podium, Brown was quickly surrounded by his Secret Service detail and rushed toward the exit.

The instant formal government is abolished, society begins to act. A general association takes place, and common interest produces common security.

Thomas Paine

All across the country, the CB radio chatter exploded.

"Break for Dallas Dave, did ya'll catch that shit on the radio… martial law has been ordered!"

"Roger that double D, Lonesome Traveler here, brother the shit is gonna hit the fan now, come back!"

"10-4 Traveler, if I know my Texas people this is gonna get bloody!"

"Yep, that's affirm Dave, word is for everyone to head for your home ports or hole up somewhere and keep your ears on."

"I heard that Travelman, I got a feeling that we are gonna be awful busy spreading the news for a while."

"That's a rog Dallas, Traveling Man out."

After watching the President's address on CSPAN from his office, Texas President Jim Walter, along with Ron Thompson,

General Joe Scott and Bill Baker sat quietly now looking at a blank TV screen. Picking up the remote control, Thompson searched the channels only to find all of them displaying test patterns; he finally turned the TV off and to no one in particular asked, "So what's our next move?"

After a moment of pause an ashen-faced Scott spoke first.

"Well we're as prepared as we can be. We're on defense, so we wait for them to make their move and react accordingly. But," he continued, "As we have been doing, we will continue to monitor the citizen band for any information from the truckers that may be useful Intel."

Thompson turned to Walter and asked "so what do you think Jim?"

Sensing a need to break the tension Walter stood up and in an exaggerated manner, stretched his arms and legs and with a wry smile replied, "I think the Cowboys need more depth at quarterback!"

Life isn't a matter of milestones, but of moments.

Rose Kennedy

Driving west on I- 30 toward Dallas, Jill and Tommy Riley had listened to the President's address and the CB chatter that followed as they made their way toward the town of Bedford to stay with relatives and wait out the developments.

"What do you think Dad, is this going to turn into an all-out civil war?"

Taking a deep breath, he replied,

"I don't know honey. I hope cooler heads will prevail, but it doesn't look very good."

"I just can't help thinking about the future," Jill sighed, "the uncertainty of what lies ahead, not just for our country but for us and me personally, is it selfish of me to think that way?"

Looking at his daughter, Tommy took her hand.

"I don't think so, we all instinctively think in our own best interests whether it's for ourselves or families, for career choices, for life and love, fear and hate, choices that we make and turns that we take, the list is endless. Life is a series of opportunities to take advantage of and obstacles to be overcome."

Jill sat silent for a moment, she had never heard he father talk like this before. It occurred to her that she had always preferred to discuss such things with her mother, and couldn't remember ever asking for his advice or council on matters of any depth. Still looking at the road ahead, she said,

"I'm sorry dad"

"For what?"

Trying to fight off the tears that now were beginning to form she replied.

"I'm ashamed of myself, I just realized that I don't know you, I always had mom to go to about such things and even after mom died I never came to you about important matters in my life. I wish we would have talked more!"

Still holding his daughter's soft hand, Tommy gave it a gentle squeeze and said,

"It's OK baby, I always had your mother to go to too. We talked about these things all the time and she would let me know how you were doing and what was going on in your life and in your heart and mind."

Unaccustomed to his own tears that were slowly rolling down his cheeks, a now-smiling Tommy Gun continued.

"I had no idea how to raise a daughter, I didn't know how to love; my father raised me to be tough and the Marines taught me to be hard, but your mother saw past all that and was able to touch that untouchable part of my heart."

Unable to control her tears, Jill listened intently, hanging on every word.

"She taught me the meaning of love, and I depended on her to impart those same qualities to you so that I could tend to my obligations of keeping a roof over our heads and putting food on the table."

Jill could only return the squeeze of her father's hand as she now found herself without any words to describe the emotions that she was feeling.

"Jill I'm so proud of you, I could not have asked for a better daughter than you. I loved your mother so much and I miss her every day. The only thing that makes her absence bearable is how much of her I see in you. I love you baby!"

Fighting off her tears, Jill continued driving until she was alerted to the warning light that had appeared on the dashboard. "CHECK ENGINE"

The fate of every democracy, of every government based on the sovereignty of the people, depends on the choices it makes between these opposite principles, absolute power on the one hand, and on the other the restraints of legality and the authority of tradition.

John Acton

President Brown and his staff sat in the Oval Office watching the BBC broadcast of the events unfolding outside of the White House.

"This is Nigel Collin reporting live for the BBC from in front of the White House in Washington, DC where a mass demonstration has begun in response to President Brown's address to the American people that imposes martial law and suspends Congress and the Constitution. Tensions are running high, and heavily armed Secret Service agents can be observed atop the White House roof as well as other positions surrounding the grounds. Additional barricades have been erected all along the perimeter fence as well as the entrance gates."

The camera then panned down Pennsylvania Avenue.

"Hundreds have already gathered and many more can be seen coming this way."

Spotting a familiar face as that of Senator Ida Mann, Collin waded into the crowd to get an interview.

"Senator Mann, what brings you out here today?"

Collin questioned as he pushed the microphone toward Mann. Surrounded by a growing number of citizens, Mann was now joined by Congressman Raginsky as well as Senators Tobin and Laflan in an impromptu news conference.

"We are here today to show support for our constituents and demonstrate our bi-partisan disapproval to the imposition of martial law and the suspension of Congressional authority," Mann replied to the cheers of the growing crowd who began to chant.

"TREASON, TREASON, TRAITOR, TRAITOR!"

"This is Nigel Collin, sending it back to our BBC studios in London."

A now outraged Brown could take no more; reaching for the first thing he could find, he stood and grabbed a solid spherical paper weight from his desk top, and with the precision of a major league pitcher threw a perfect fastball strike through the TV screen. Shocked by this episode of anger, an eerie silence fell over the room. One minute was followed by another, by yet another, time seemed to stand still. Sitting quietly with his head in his hands Meyer Epstein had finally had enough! He stood and announced,

"Mr. President, against all my political advice you have pursued this course of action that has led this administration to disaster! I therefore formally tender my resignation, effective immediately." He swiftly walked out of the room, slamming the door behind him.

Brown fell back into his chair; his outrage had now turned to complete shock! Epstein had been his closest and most trusted advisor and now he was gone. During his entire political career Brown had never felt this alone! Again the silence was deafening. Then…

"Mr. President," came the voice over the intercom,

"General Crain is on the line." An exasperated Brown took a deep breath before pushing the button to activate the speaker.

"Yes George."

"Mr. President, I don't like what I'm seeing on the BBC. I would like to, with your permission, dispatch an armored unit of M1-A1 Abrams battle tanks with support of infantry units to set up a defensive perimeter around the White House compound to support your Secret Service detail, as well as a squadron of AH-64 Apache helicopters ready to be deployed as a show of force to act as a deterrent to any escalation of these protests. In order to do this, I would need the permission of the Secret Service to land one Apache on the White House lawn that would be at the ready to quickly, if needed, serve as Air Force One, while three others fly low level passes over the compound and the crowd. This also requires permission to enter restricted air space."

"Permission granted George and thank you."

Nigel Collin was continuing to record interviews of protesters when the sound of the slash of the Apache's helicopter blades could be heard approaching in the distance.

"London, GO LIVE, GO LIVE NOW!" Cupping his earpiece, BBC London Anchorman Edward Reginald paused his report.

"We now go back live to Nigel Collin in America. Nigel what do you have for us?"

Just in time to catch the approaching aircraft the camera panned toward the sky.

"Edward we have a stunning new development. I count four heavily armed military helicopters flying overhead, and one appears to be landing on the White House lawn. The remaining three buzzed the crowd and have now gained altitude and taken up hovering stationary positions above the White House itself."

The crowd had quieted to this turn of events when suddenly there was a different noise, a mechanical sound much like the sound of…

"TANKS!" Collin yelled.

The camera now panned down to street level where the crowd was now parting like Moses parting the Red Sea to reveal the awesome sight of the approaching Abrams battle tanks followed by troop transport vehicles. The tanks and troops began taking up defensive positions all along the fence perimeter around the compound. After some minutes, an officer stepped out of a jeep and looked around. Seeing that everything was in place, he radioed in.

"Forward position to base, area is secure."

Battles are won by slaughter and maneuver. The greater the general, the more he contributes in maneuver, the less he demands in slaughter.

Winston Churchill

Reading through his daily briefing reports from Bill Baker, General Joe Scott spotted something that piqued his interest. It seemed that while the intelligence service was monitoring CB chatter by truckers for anything that could be used as information, a repeated call was being made from Cary Grant to Virginia Lee for a traffic update without any response. Using a secure line, Scott immediately called Baker.

"Bill, can you come down to my office?"

"Yes sir, I'm just down the hall." Within minutes Baker arrived. "What's up Joe?"

"Did you see this CB transmission?"

"Yeah, our communications and intelligence people don't know what to make of it. Why?"

"I'm not sure, but I have a funny feeling. Let's go down there and try something."

With that Scott and Baker made their way toward the elevator that would take them down to the second lower level, where the communications center was located. At first glance, Scott was amazed at the amount of sophistication that was being employed to monitor land line and cell phone traffic, as well as the internet and the citizen band radio. Working their way through the room Scott and Baker finally found the station where a young lady was sitting monitoring the CB chatter.

"What's your name?" he asked.

"Janet."

Showing her the transcript, he asked

"Did you report this?"

"Yes sir, it comes in about every five minutes, does it mean something?"

"I don't know, let's find out."

Finding a pen and a piece of paper to write on, Scott scribbled something and said,

"Send this reply next time it comes through." After a few minutes came the request.

"Cary Grant to Virginia Lee for a traffic report OVER."

Janet replied. "Virginia Lee to Cary Grant, can you point me in the right direction OVER." The response came back quickly.

"All points west OVER."

Again Scott scribbled on the paper and handed it to Janet, "send this."

Doing as she was told Janet keyed the mic,

"All clear from Boise to where? OVER"

"All the way to the Golden Gates OVER."

"Tell him 10-4ski. I'll be damned," Scott said out loud.

"You know what this is Joe?" Baker asked.

"Yeah, it's Crain trying to communicate with me; it's a code we made up that only he and I understand." Scott explained.

"When we were cadets together at West Point, we would play all different kinds of war games and debate the Civil War. He was Ulysses S. Grant and I was Robert E. Lee, and Lee was from Virginia." Scott continued.

"He was born in Boise and his family moved to San Francisco."

A short pause was followed by,

"Unnatural forces being consumed at the lobster's claw, wounds my heart, OVER." Puzzled, Baker shrugging his shoulders and looked at Scott. Thinking for a moment Scott said…

"He's telling us that he has identified our soft spot and understands the strategy, so he's deploying expendable UN troops to invade there tomorrow."

"I don't get it," Baker replied.

Scott explained. "Well the first two letters of 'unnatural forces' would stand for United Nations troops, consumed means he considers them as expendable. A lobster's claw is a pincer, which is our strategy." Again Scott scribbled on the paper and gave it to Janet. "Send that." A strange look came across Janet's face as she read what he had written and looked back at Scott. Now becoming impatient, he emphatically pointed his finger at the radio. "Send it!" Doing as instructed, Janet keyed the mic.

"With a monotonous languor, OVER." The response was immediate.

"Roger that."

Before he was asked, Scott continued his explanation.

"Wound my heart with a monotonous languor' was what the BBC signaled to the French Resistance, that the invasion would begin within hours. The French then set about destroying German targets to pave the way for invasion at Normandy." The transmission continued.

"Spotted dogs with wagging tails at frogs landing above the Jesus Sea, join Red Juan's beach party OVER."

A momentary look of confusion crossed Scott's face, but within a minute he demanded.

"I need a map of Texas!"

After what seemed like an hour, a map was delivered and General Joe Scott began to survey the landscape.

"Ok, I got it," he declared. Looking Baker right in the eye he said, "spotted dogs' are Dalmatians, which means 101

Dalmatians or 101st airborne paratroopers. 'With wagging tails' means that they are friendly."

Scott continued decoding the message. "This precedes an amphibious, indicated by 'frogs,' invasion landing force by 'Red Juan,' the 1st infantry division known as the Big Red One landing on the beach above or north of the Jesus Sea, which would mean Corpus Christi bay." Scott again pointed to Janet.

"Roger that OVER."

"Why is Crain giving us this Intel Joe?" Baker questioned. The answer came before Scott could respond.

"Blooming flowers in 168 chimes, Cary Grant OUT!"

Hearing this Scott's face turned completely pale and his expression turned to that of sheer horror as he replied with only three words.

"Oh my God."

"What is it Joe?"

Finding the nearest empty chair, General Joe Scott slowly sat and put his head in his hands and muttered

"What have we done?"

A dead silence now filled the room. Minutes passed like hours, finally a concerned Baker asked,

"General, are you alright?"

A now teary-eyed Joe Scott raised his head and looked up at the astonished face of Colonel Baker. As solemnly as if he were delivering a eulogy for an old friend, he began.

"Flowers bloom in May, and 168 chimes mean 168 hours or seven days. It's a reference to a movie, Seven Days in May about an attempted coup by the US military."

His mouth now agape, Baker could only blankly stare ahead before asking,

"What are your orders General?"

"Repel at soft spot, take no action near Corpus Christi!"

CHAPTER FIFTEEN

The way to love anything is to realize that it may be lost.

Gilbert K. Chesterton

LEAVING ATT STADIUM, HIS MISSION NOW COMPLETE, Dennis felt a sense of accomplishment as well as relief, and the thought of relaxing by the pool for a few days was quickly becoming a good idea as a way to clear his head. Following the directions he was given by the stadium clerk, Coleman back-tracked east on I-30, then north on TX-360 north toward the town of Bedford. He then turned onto Airport Freeway and followed the signs in the direction of DFW airport that would lead to the Holiday Inn.

Dennis began to contemplate his options. *Would he stay in Texas and begin a new life and try to become a small part of the birth of a new nation that which more resembled what the founding fathers had intended America to be? Or choose to go back to Chicago and resume what life he had there, if, under the circumstances, that were even a possibility?* Questioning himself, he considered. *What did he really have there? He had no family and few close friends. He lived alone in a mundane existence, in a dead end job with no future, working as a mechanic for a company that had no respect for its employees and treated its customers and its suppliers badly, in a country that no longer allowed its people to be free to pursue their happiness as they saw fit.*

Dennis was not by any means an old man, but not exactly a young man either. He felt like he was approaching an important crossroads in more ways than one. If he decided to stay, maybe he would meet someone and finally settle down and start a family of his own. If only he could meet a loving, caring woman that shared not only his values, but also could understand his occasional sarcasms and warped sense of humor. The thought that he was setting his sights too high reminded him of an old joke. Now how did that go?

To be happy, a man needs to find a woman that is a good cook, a woman who is a good mother, a woman that keeps a clean house, and a woman who is good in bed. But the most important thing is that these four women never meet!

Laughing to himself, Dennis let the momentary amusement subside before again resuming serious thought. *Loving wife, comfortable home, children to play with and raise, who knows, maybe he could even pursue his ambition to start his own business, to be his own boss, and set his own schedule.* He wondered *were these obtainable goals or merely pipe dreams with too many obstacles to overcome?*

Back and forth, Dennis's mind was now racing, from his conversation with the man on the CB and Jeff Davis assuring him that he would make the right decision and advising him to get some rest. His thoughts now returned to Jill. *Maybe this would be a good time to call her.*

As if he was struck by a bullet he suddenly realized he had given the receipt stub with her phone number on it to the clerk at ATT Stadium. *God damn it, now he would have to turn around and go back there to retrieve that stub!*

Just as Dennis was about to turn back, he spotted a truck broken down on the roadside shoulder and decided to see if he could be of assistance.

Steam now streaming from the engine of the old pick up, Jill had carefully pulled off to the side of the road. Removing her tired body from behind the wheel, she lifted the hood to see what the trouble was. Waving her hands to try and clear out the steaming smoke, she could see that antifreeze was dripping from a small hole in the hose near the radiator. *"Shit"* she thought.

"What's wrong honey?" asked her father, joining her.

Exasperated, Jill sighed.

"There's a hole in the radiator hose and the radiator is dry, it looks like we're going to need a mechanic."

As if an answer to a yet unspoken prayer, just then another pickup had pulled in behind them.

"Thank you God," she said aloud as she waved to the driver.

"Do you know anything about engines?" she asked. A tall man got out and was walking toward them, as they approached one another, Jill thought he looked familiar.

Hardly able to see through the steam, all Dennis could make out were the figures of a woman and an older man coming toward him. Raising his voice so as to be heard above the noise of the traffic he asked,

"You need some help?"

Once the distance between them closed to within a few feet, instantly they recognized each other and stopped dead in their tracks. As if he were trying to snap out of a dream, Dennis gave his head a quick shake and in amazement said,

"You're Jill."

Her heart began to pound, but managing to nod, Jill was speechless and not able to believe her eyes. She could only stare at the man's face. Her pulse was now racing. *He remembered my name.*

Embarrassed and now blushing, not knowing what to say, a tongue-tied Jill finally managed,

"And you're two eggs up with bacon, hash browns and white toast."

The irony of the awkward moment struck them and they both began to laugh.

"I was just going to call you."

A skeptical Jill replied, "I thought maybe you lost the number."

"I did, I was just on my way back to find it" Dennis said sheepishly. Extending his hand to introduce himself, he said…

"I'm Dennis Coleman."

Taking his hand, "I'm Jill Riley and this is my father Tommy."

Now able to break his gaze away from Jill, Dennis looked at Tommy for the first time. He immediately recognized the ball cap with the eagle and American flag.

"And you're the man at the diner," he said, shaking his head.

Offering his right hand to Dennis, Tommy said.

"Glad to meet ya son."

Taking Tommy's hand, Dennis was amazed by the firmness of the man's grip, but returned it with equal strength.

"Wait a minute, you're Tommy Gun Riley! You and I talked on the CB, I'm Goldilocks."

Not saying a word but still holding Coleman's hand, Tommy Gun looked into the face of his daughter, then back at Dennis. He smiled and said,

"Well son, it looks like God put you where you needed to be when you needed to be there! Now let's get this truck fixed and get on with our lives!"

The idea of aerial military surveillance dates back to the Civil War, when both the Union and the Confederacy used hot-air balloons to spy on the other side, tracking troop movements and helping to direct artillery fire.

Michael Hastings

Scanning the terrain with binoculars for several hours, forward observer PFC Daniel Braverman of the Texas Guard spied the bridge that crossed the Neches River north of

Beaumont before he spotted the column of U.N. armor and infantry crossing into Texas. He signaled his communications operator to radio the status to the gun batteries.

"Forward observer to battery one, be advised, enemy forces crossing target in great strength, hold fire!"

Braverman continued to observe until the full force had crossed before giving the order to the artillery units.

"Battery one, fire!"

With that, one Howitzer let loose a single round. Hearing the ungodly roar of the 105 MM shell whistling through the air above, Braverman watched intently as the shot hit long and slightly left of its target.

"Forward observer to battery one, heavy 20 meters, adjust 10 right."

The booming blare of another single round shrieked overhead, resulting in a direct hit right in the center of the bridge.

"Forward observer to battery one, target destroyed!"

Braverman now turned his attention to the scattering armor units.

"Batteries one and two, adjust fire to grid reference three, fire!"

Within seconds the frightful thunder of the barrage was deafening, even at this distance. From his perched position atop hill E 25-17, Braverman continued to monitor the round placement and directed fire. He could feel the ground shaking below him as he watched the enemy forces frantically seeking cover; they appeared to be in complete disarray!

"Batteries one and two, on target, continue fire, adjust fire accordingly. Mobile armor units advance and fire at will."

Seeing they had no retreat across the Neches, the U.N. infantry attempted to pivot to the south, only to find that they were flanked by units of the Texas Guard and militia that were now laying out small arms fire that was decimating their ranks.

An astonished Braverman felt as if he were watching a movie as he witnessed the carnage that was happening before his eyes. What was left of the U.N. armor now turned north-ward in an attempt to spearhead a breakout through the northern flank, only to be out-maneuvered and outnumbered by the Russian built T-72's.

"Forward observer to rear guard units, close in."

As ordered, Texas ground forces immediately rushed in behind from both flanks and closed the pincer. Realizing their predicament, Braverman watched as the ground forces began to lay down their arms and drop to the ground, while all that was left of the enemy's armor stopped in their tracks and lowered their guns to signal surrender.

"Forward observer to all units, cease fire!"

I don't think that my kind of journalism has ever been universally popular. It's lonely out here.

Hunter S. Thompson

Back in Washington, a stunned President Brown, along with Vice President Tom Terry and Secretary of Defense Robert Creighton, monitored the scene from the White House situation room.

"This is Charles Thomas reporting for the BBC from northeastern Texas, where United Nations forces have been routed in an attempted invasion of the breakaway American state. It appears that although equipment losses are heavy, human casualties are minimal with reports of a few dozen soldiers wounded and only two KIA battlefield casualties. Back to you in London, Edward."

"Thank you Charles, we now take you live to Jonathan Giles, what do you have for us?"

"Edward, I'm aboard a U.S. Army 8 class LCM landing craft imbedded with American 1st Infantry division landing forces, approaching the beach south of Corpus Christie, Texas. About two dozen crafts have already landed ahead of us; the soldiers have hit the beach and are advancing inland without any resistance whatsoever."

Giles continued his report, "Apache attack helicopters and C-130 transports have over flown our position and the canopies of paratroopers and equipment can be seen descending to the north."

I look forward to a great future for America - a future in which our country will match its military strength with our moral restraint, its wealth with our wisdom, its power with our purpose.

John F. Kennedy

General Joseph Scott and Colonel Bill Baker sat watching the BBC broadcast from the communications room.

"Forward guards to base, paratroops and infantry have landed without incident. Please confirm continued rules of engagement – over."

"Rules of engagement confirmed; do not fire unless fired upon – over," came the reply.

"Roger that base, forward guard out."

Turning to Scott, Baker asked,

"Joe, are you absolutely sure of Crain's intentions?"

"I'm sure Bill. Look at it like this. He correctly identified our strategy at Beaumont and communicated it to us, he employed U.N. forces that he considered as expendable to that action knowing that I would respond by repelling that force and that it would send the message that we will engage with an invading force. Then he let us know that U.S forces will land at the designated area; that they are loyal to him and sympathetic to our cause so we should take no action to engage them. Are you with me so far?"

"I'm with you," Baker replied, nodding.

"Knowing me the way he does, he knows that this would give us strategic advantage and two options. One, we let them advance inland to link up with paratroopers to a point that would enable us to close in from both flanks and the rear and surround them; thus forcing their surrender. Or two, we overwhelm them with superior numbers in case it's an elaborate ruse. He also knows that this would not be reported by the controlled American media, so he's using one of the world's most respected news agencies, the BBC, to report it to the rest of the world." Baker just stared in amazement.

"It's brilliant. The only thing I don't know is how he intends to play out the Seven Days in May scenario," concluded Scott. The two men sat silently for a moment.

"I do have one question though. When you and Crain played these war games together, who won?"

Lowering his head as if in shame, sadly Scott replied,

"He did."

And upon this act, sincerely believed to be an act of justice, warranted by the Constitution, upon military necessity, I invoke the considerate judgment of all mankind, and the gracious favor of Almighty God.

Salmon P. Chase

From the Situation Room, President Brown and Vice President Terry continued to monitor what they hoped would be a decisive battle that would end this conflict once and for all. With his thick Welsh accent, BBC anchorman Reginald continued his broadcast.

"This is Edward Reginald reporting from our London bureau where we have been monitoring developments in the American breakaway state of Texas. Let's go back now to Jonathan Giles. Tell us what is happening Jonathan."

"Well Edward, as I reported earlier, the U.S. 1st Infantry Division forces have successfully landed without any resistance or incident, and advanced northward and are now linking up with elements of the 101st airborne paratrooper units. Squadrons of Texas air guard F/A 18 super hornets can be seen flying overhead and look to be preparing to engage the Apaches. We have reports that the Texas Guard and citizen's militia have halted their retreat approximately one mile ahead and appear to be readying to make a stand against a frontal assault."

The supreme art of war is to subdue the enemy without fighting.

Sun Tzu

Brown and Terry continued to watch the BBC report as they waited for the battle to begin and put an end to this rebellion of his authority. Hardly able to contain his delight, *finally he would realize his dreams to succeed where so many others before him had failed, and be recognized as the leader of a new world order and cement his place in history!*

Just then, an excited Jonathan Giles exclaimed,

"Wait, something is happening! It appears that the U.S. Apache helicopters are landing and refusing to provide air cover for the invasion forces who are now laying down their arms signaling surrender!"

Suddenly realizing he had been double crossed, Brown's elation quickly turned to that of utter discouragement. Looking around the room, Brown searched for the one person he could depend on, Meyer Epstein. Now, at the time he needed Epstein to advise him the most, he was not available; he hadn't returned any of the messages Brown had left since his resignation.

Breaking the silence that had engulfed the room, Vice President Terry spoke.

"Mr. President we have been set up. You need to fire General Crain immediately!" Brown could only nod his head slowly in agreement.

Comfortably seated in overstuffed chairs outside of the Oval Office, along with his adjutant Colonel Alan Kramer, General George Crain sat patiently and checked his watch when the President's secretary's phone rang.

"Yes Mr. President." Listening for a moment she replied,

"General Crain is already here sir." Another brief moment of silence was followed by the same response. "Yes Mr. President."

Gesturing toward Crain she said "You may go in now General."

Standing up, Crain, in rigid military fashion, straightened his uniform jacket and again checked his watch, looked at Kramer and said, "Well, here we go!"

Upon entering the Oval Office, Crain was met by a stern-faced Brown standing before the Resolute desk. Walking straight up to Brown, Crain stood at attention. Infuriated, Brown screamed,

"Just what the fuck is going on here George?"

Crain checked his watch, thirty seconds.

"I don't know what you mean sir; I followed your directives to the letter."

"Then why have your forces surrendered?"

"Did I, or did I not warn you of the possibility that they would refuse to fight sir?" Crain shot back. Fifteen seconds.

"Then why did you use U.N. TROOPS to attack at the Neches River bridge?" asked Brown.

"Because I knew they would fight sir," Crain said, again checking his watch. Ten seconds.

"Knowing full well that it was a trap, and that the Texas defenses would overwhelm them?" Brown questioned.

Still standing at attention, he replied "Yes Sir.!"

"Why?" Brown challenged.

"Because sir, you have completely exceeded your authority as President and failed to uphold your oath of office, Sir."

"Crain, you're fired!" Yelled an irate Brown.

"I'm afraid you have it backwards sir, you're fired." Crain countered.

Three, two, one, zero…Crain gestured toward the television monitor to hear Nigel Collin break in.

"London go live, something's happening here!"

The cameras panned to record the sight of the Abrams battle tanks rotating their turrets and pointing their guns directly at the White House. Simultaneously they advanced over and though the fences, followed by infantry foot soldiers who were rushing in from behind. Perched upon the White House roof, Secret Service Service agents responded with small arms fire down on the soldiers who were laying siege to the White House itself. Now taking up attack positions, the Apache helicopters strafed the rooftop Secret Service agents until they obeyed the order to surrender that came from a loud speaker aboard one of the hovering helicopters.

Looking back at Brown, Crain said,

"It would seem the game has changed sir."

"You're seizing control of the government?" Brown shot back in distain.

"As usual sir, you have things backwards. It was you who seized control of the government. Your executive order to abolish the elected Congress and the Supreme Court, and initiate martial law was the definition of a coup d'état. That order also gave me the authority over all branches of the military, as well as all government agencies and all state and local law enforcement to implement and enforce it."

Watching his dreams disintegrate before his eyes, in total despair Brown demanded,

"How can you do this to me George?"

"You made it easy for me sir. You gave the orders, and I followed them, and by my actions today to suppress the coup, I remain true to the oath that I took when I first put on this uniform; to defend the Constitution of the United States against all enemies, foreign, and in this case sir, domestic. Sir you are under arrest!"

As if readying to absorb a heavy blow, Brown straightening himself, said,

"I demand to know the charges!"

Crain replied in kind, "Treason, sedition, conspiracy to commit treason, and violation of your oath of office. You have my word that you will be given an adequate defense during your impeachment and trial, and that no harm shall come to your family."

His ego now shattered into so many pieces, a no longer arrogant Omar Brown realized his predicament and accepted defeat. He hung his head saying,

"I thank you for that General."

Turning to Kramer, Crain gave the order.

"Colonel, take Mr. Brown and Mr. Terry into custody."

"Edward Reginald reporting live from BBC studios in London that a military takeover of the United States government has taken place, we now return you to Nigel Collin on the scene in front of the White House in Washington D.C. Nigel what's the latest?"

"Edward, this was the scene recorded moments ago as President Brown and Vice President Terry were led by armed military guards to an awaiting helicopter to be flown to an undisclosed location. We have just been given a prepared statement that reads that the seizure of power by the administration has been put down by the military, and that President Brown, along with all the members of his cabinet, have been placed under arrest, and that chairman of the Joint Chiefs, General George Crain, will address the nation and the rest of the world this evening."

A politician thinks of the next election. A statesman, of the next generation.

James Freeman Clarke

As if sitting on pins and needles, Texas President Jim Walter, along with Ron Thompson, General Joe Scott and Bill Baker, gathered in Walter's office and nervously awaited Crain's address. Sensing the growing tension, Walter poured coffee, handed a cup to each man, and said,

"Take it easy guys, just breath normally."

This simple remark seemed to produce the needed calming effect as each man smiled and sipped their coffee. The quiet was soon broken by the distinctly British accent of Nigel Collin.

"Ladies and gentleman, General Crain will now give his address."

Flanked by American flags on both sides, a stern-faced Crain stepped up to the podium and began.

"My fellow citizens, and all those watching around the world, I speak to you tonight with mixed emotions and a heavy heart. Today we have taken the necessary steps to put down a conspiracy to seize power by the leaders of the current administration. Though it is legally within the authority of the President to issue this type of executive order, an action of this type is to only be taken in the event of national disaster or crisis. Since no such crisis or disaster existed, President Brown exceeded that authority to create one, for the purpose of seizing power and unifying all control to himself and his administration, by abolishing Congress and the Supreme Court. This created the Constitutional crisis that was required to initiate martial law and employ the military to enforce it. In doing this the President, along with Vice President Terry and members of his cabinet and United Nation officials, conspired to attempt what by definition was a civilian coup d'état. The actions undertaken by US military forces today to put down this coup were also legal; however, the military will remain in control until such time as steps are taken to restore civilian control of the government. Martial law remains in effect."

" The President and all other known coconspirators have been taken into custody and will be detained at the military prison at Guantanamo Bay, Cuba until a new Congress is elected by the people, who will then select and seat a new Supreme Court, who will conduct impeachment hearings and trials. Elections will be held in the normal lawful manner with the following exceptions; due to conflict of interest, lawyers and members of the bar will be ineligible to hold office in the legislative and executive branches. Elections will be subject to strict monitoring by the military. Only U.S. citizens will be eligible to vote, and must show proof of citizenship. Voter fraud will be punishable with a minimum of ten years confinement. As is constitutionally required by rules of succession, the Speaker of the House will assume the Presidency, but remain under the direction of the interterm military government until such time as an election is held to elect a new President."

Crain paused to take a breath before continuing.

"Other actions taken today are as follows. First, as a result of implementation of martial law, our military status automatically elevated to DEFCON 2. In response, Russia and China responded in kind. I have since ordered our defense condition lowered to DEFCON 3, and both Russia and China have followed suit. Second, I have assured our NATO allies that our treaties will remain in place, and the United States shall honor our commitments. Third, I have ordered all of our borders to be secured and all immigration to be suspended until new policies shall be implemented by the newly elected Congress. Any person or persons that attempt to enter the U.S. illegally will be considered hostile intruders and dealt with accordingly. Any person currently holding, or wishing to obtain, visas will be required to reapply and will comply to close monitoring or face permanent expulsion. Fourth, the national news media, including free and cable television, the internet, and print will be free to report the news, but shall refrain from offering personal opinions. Journalists who wish to speak their opinions are free to exercise their First Amendment right to do so as private citizens. Fifth, all wages and prices are hereby frozen at current levels. Assets of all U.S. financial institutions and U.S corporations, as well as stock and commodities exchanges are also hereby frozen. Regular trade and commerce shall continue as normal, however, any foreign corporations or financial institutions that attempt to take advantage of these restrictions shall result in the imposition of strict tariffs, up to and including seizure of those assets. All foreign aid is hereby suspended until the new civilian government is seated and our national debt is under control. However, the U.S. shall respond to render aid of emergency food, medical assistance or supplies, etc. to any disaster areas in need. Sixth, as a result of the complicity of the United Nations in the attempted coup, I have ordered the expulsion of the U.N. from the United States, and the immediate withdrawal of our delegation from that institution. Last, but not least, to our brothers and sisters of Texas. The United States of America offers its friendship, and will recognize your right to remain a free and sovereign state, or to rejoin the union, and look forward toward reestablishing relations and commerce in our common interests. In conclusion, we ask for calm and patience as we undertake the processes to make this transition to reestablishing the dream of the great nation that our founding fathers envisioned. God Bless the United States of America!"

CHAPTER SIXTEEN

Never in the field of human conflict was so much owed by so many to so few.

Winston Churchill

A GENTLE BREEZE BLEW THROUGH THE LEAVES OF the Oak trees that lined the banks of the Little River in Bell County, as Texas President Jim Walter tightened his line and lay back to relax. Taking a deep breath of the clean crisp air, while searching for a cloud, he could find nothing but a clear blue sky. He was reminded of the long ago days of his care-free youth, when he and Ron Thompson would sit quietly for hours on end, fishing for that prized catch that would give one of them bragging rights over the other.

It had been a little over four years ago when he and Ron had first contemplated making this trip together. *My God had it been that long?* he thought. It sometimes seemed like longer, but other times only yesterday. A familiar noise broke his concentration. Looking over his shoulder, he could see Ron busy baiting his hook and checking the drag on his favorite reel before making his cast.

"Don't cross my line" Walter warned, knowing that he would, just to aggravate him.

Not looking at Walter, in an exaggerated tone Thompson replied, "Fuck you."

"Is that any way to speak to your President?" retorted Walter with equal sarcasm.

"You're right," Thompson shot back. "Fuck you, Mr. President, SIR!"

The juvenile-natured banter caused them both to let out a heartfelt belly laugh they had not felt for many years. Finally Thompson asked,

"Where are you?"

"Straight out, about ten yards," Walter replied.

Reaching for his thermos, he poured himself a cup of steaming coffee and returned to his thoughts. *So much had happened during the last four years*, he thought. *We've come a long way to get to this point, establishing our own nation, revising our Constitution and laws pertaining to our own self-governance, developing our own economy and relations with other countries, and so many other things on a seemingly endless list that he thought it would never end.*

Holding his fishing pole in one hand and the coffee in the other, he took a sip from his cup as he felt a heavy tug on his line. Quickly setting the cup down he sat up just in time to see Thompson frantically reeling in his last cast.

"Damn it, I just told you not to cross my line!" Walter scolded.

Not saying a word, Thompson refused to look at Walter, but it was apparent that he was pleased with himself, going by the shit-eating grin that he could see from his profile as he continued to reel in his line. Both men reeled in their lines to reveal a tangled mess of fishing line and stick weed. Again Walter began his scolding,

"I told you…"

"Let me use your pocket knife," said Thompson, cutting Walter off in mid-sentence.

Reaching into his vest pocket, Walter searched for his trusty Buck Old Timer knife when… "Oww!"

A sharp pain shot through his hand! Jumping up from his prone position, Walter quickly pulled his hand from his pocket to reveal a crawdad that Thompson had slipped in there. It had attached itself to his middle finger and was hanging on for dear life. Thompson bellowed with laughter watching his friend jumping around waving his extended middle finger in a futile effort to dislodge the offending crustacean yelling, "Son of a bitch!"

Finally, after prying it free from his now swelling appendage, a still laughing Ron Thompson asked,

"Can we quote you on that Mr. President?"

Walter shot him a dirty look before he also burst out laughing at his own stupidity for again falling for that same old gag. Settling back down, Jim Walter poured himself another cup of coffee to replace what had spilled during his epic crawdad battle, and reached into the bag that contained the sweet rolls that Barbara Rae had packed for them. He removed a bear claw and threw the bag at his friend.

"Cheese Danish?" Thompson asked, as he reached in the bag. He smiled as he pulled out a second bear claw.

"See, you still care," deadpanned Thompson.

"Shut up and untangle my line."

Again smiling to himself, Texas President Jim Walter thought, *nothing beats the company of old friend.*

Love is our true destiny. We do not find the meaning of life by ourselves alone - we find it with another.

Thomas Merton

Hearing the sound of tires braking on gravel, the old man's attention returned to the window just in time to see the welcome sight of the pickup truck as it came to a stop. A familiar sign decorated the driver's door that read, **Coleman Mechanical Maintenance and Repair.** The old man continued to focus on the driver as he exited the vehicle and strode toward the entrance with his younger companion in tow. Upon hearing the ringing sound of the bell mounted above the door that signaled a customer's arrival to the Foreman Diner, Jed and Clarence turned to give the man a welcoming wave and a friendly "Good morning" and immediately returned to their pigskin prognostications.

Returning the wave, Dennis Coleman and his partner turned to the right and strolled toward the old man seated at their favorite table as they took their regular seats.

"Morning Dad."

"Good morning," Tommy Gun greeted them both.

Within seconds their waitress appeared with a tray full of plates of food. Taking great care to properly place them, she carefully distributed the meals. "Biscuits and gravy" for dad, "two eggs up, hash browns, bacon and white toast" for Dennis.

"And for the birthday boy," Jill Coleman proudly announced,

"Blueberry pancakes with whipped cream on top." She placed the plate in front of a grinning little Tommy Coleman.

Taking her seat next to her father, Jill leaned over to light the three candles that adorned the top of the short stack and began to sing. Temporarily leaving his kitchen duties, Billy Joe, along with Jed and Clarence, came over to join in the singing celebration.

"Happy birthday dear Tommy…happy birthday to you!" Smiling from ear to ear, little Tommy made a wish, took a deep breath and extinguished the flames with a single blow.

EPILOGUE

The American Dream is a term that is often used but also often misunderstood. It isn't really about becoming rich or famous. It is about things much simpler and more fundamental than that.

Marco Rubio

His hunger now satisfied, Dennis Coleman pushed his chair back away from the table and sat back in his seat to stretch out his torso. Looking to his left, his gaze fell upon the sight of Jill as she walked toward them, coffee pot in hand. Locking eyes with those of her husband, Jill smiled broadly as she approached. Across the table sat a man who was not just his father-in-law, but had become his dad. Looking beyond him through the window, he could see the business sign that decorated the door of his pickup. To his right sat his three year old son, still happily devouring his birthday treat.

At that moment, Dennis could not have been any happier. *This was it he thought; his pursuit of happiness was now complete. He was living the American Dream!*

THE END

ACKNOWLEDGMENTS

All my friends and relatives who encouraged me to finish this story

Thanks to my niece Jeannie Shay and Dennis Bingham for their editing work and advice.

Bob and Nora Phalon, Norine Dalton and Jean Marie

Special thanks to my son Jim for his cover artwork.

The History Channel.

John Wayne Movies, Tom Clancy and Louis L'Amour whose writing styles I tried desperately to mimic.

The music of Frank Sinatra that I endlessly listened to while writing.

REFERENCES

Wikipedia

HMS Resolute was a mid-19th-century barque-rigged ship of the British Royal Navy, specially outfitted for Arctic exploration. Resolute became trapped in the ice and was abandoned. Recovered by an American whaler, she was returned to Queen Victoria in 1856. Timbers from the ship were later used to construct a desk which was then presented to the President of the United States.

Mapquest.com, Militaryfactory.com, Globalsecurity. org, Truckcountry.com, the History Channel and the Military Channel.

Brainyquotes.com, Thomas Jefferson, William S. Burroughs, Winston Churchill, H. L. Mencken, John Wayne, Lord Acton, Sam Houston, Robert Frost, Frank Lloyd Wright, Denis Waitley, Sinclair Lewis Book – It Can't Happen Here, My Way - Frank Sinatra, Charles de Gaulle, Movie - The Shootist, Louis L'Amour, Tom Clancy, Clarence Darrow, Pericles, Mark Twain, Buddha, P.J. O'Rourke, Vince Lombardi, Movie – Deliverance, George S. Patton, William Westmoreland, Hunter

S. Thompson, Nikola Tesla, John F. Kennedy, Henry Ward Beecher, Ronald Reagan, Mother Teresa, Sebastian Junger, Euripides, Chris Kyle, Henry Miller, Ambrose Bieree, Jeane Kirkpatrick, Woodrow Wilson, Aristotle, Jonathan Swift, Ayn Rand, Thomas Paine, Rose Kennedy, Movie – 101 Dalmatians, Movie – Seven Days in May, Gilbert K. Chesterton, Michael Hastings, Salmon P. Chase, Sun Tzu, James Freeman Clarke, Thomas Merton, Marco Rubio